Moonlight and Mistletoe

Marcia Lynn McClure

Published by Distractions Ink
1290 Mirador Loop N.E.
Rio Rancho, NM 87144

Published by Distractions Ink
©Copyright 2019 by M. Meyers
A.K.A. Marcia Lynn McClure
Cover Photography by ©Vian1980/Dreamstime.com
Cover Design and Interior Graphics by Sandy Ann Allred/Timeless Allure

First Printed Edition: May 2019
First Hardcover Edition: May 2019

All character names and personalities in this work of fiction are entirely
fictional, created solely in the imagination of the author. Any resemblance
to any person living or dead is coincidental.

McClure, Marcia Lynn, 1965—
Moonlight and Mistletoe: a novel/by Marcia Lynn McClure.

ISBN: 978-1-7330336-0-2

Library of Congress Control Number:

Printed in the United States of America

To **ANYONE** anywhere who needs a
dreamy, easy, romantic escape!
It's not Dusty Britches,
It's not the Ipswiches.
But here's hoping dear Roger will keep you in stitches!

Read on to meet Roger!
Also, I dreamt this corny dedication, and it wouldn't get out of my
head! My apologies for ever-increasing goofiness!

CHAPTER ONE

Adelaide Plume closed her eyes for a moment, savoring the refreshing breeze and the soothing scents of dust, cattle, leather, and horses. She listened for a moment as well—listened to the sounds of the lingering autumn birds chirruping high in the heavy branches of the cottonwoods. She could hear the cowboys whistling commands to their horses and the cattle they were herding—the quiet yet argumentative bawl of a few disobedient heifers.

Adelaide opened her eyes, smiling as she returned her attention to the cowboys cutting the herd. It was a marvelous October day adorned with warm sunshine and all the sights, sounds, and smells she loved most about her family's cattle ranch. Indeed, she felt blessed to be living out west instead of east somewhere in a big city. Although in all her seventeen years on the earth she'd never been to any city bigger than Santa Fe, Adelaide exhaled a heavy sigh of pure contentment, musing that she felt sorry for big city folk. How could folks endure living amongst rows and rows of shops and other buildings in those bustling, busy cities? How could they breathe when there was no plush green pasture grass stretching out forever before the beauty of rugged, majestic mountains on the horizon? Adelaide could not even imagine how much city folks missed—whether they knew it or not. And she didn't care if it was 1892 and

1

both coasts of the United States of America were teaming with people and progress. She loved the wide-open space that was a rancher's life in Colorado. She loved the far horizon, the cattle, the small town three miles down the road.

"Golly!" Janie exclaimed in a near whisper, drawing Adelaide's attention from her happy reveries. "That new cowboy yer pop and daddy hired sure is good-lookin'."

Still smiling, Adelaide nodded as she gazed at her pop's new hire. "As handsome as they come, I reckon," she agreed.

"I mean, just look at the way he rides!" Janie noted. "Pert'n near gives your brother Harvey a run for his money, I'd say. The boy sits a saddle like he was born onto it!"

"Mm-hmm, he sure does," Adelaide sighed with admiration. Handsome cowboys were another thing city folks did without— poor devils. Shaking her head, Adelaide mumbled to herself, "They don't know what they're missin'."

For what Janie had said was true. The new cowhand Adelaide's father and grandfather had hired to winter on the ranch surely was a sight to see. He made her glad that three of their regular hands had decided to winter with their own families that year. Because if there ever were a tall drink of water to put Adelaide's heart to thumping, it was Chance Flannery. She smiled as she watched the good-looking man cutting a smaller nearby herd. He was weeding out the group of Mr. Worden's heifers that had escaped through a damaged portion of fence line and were now mixed in with her daddy and pop's herd. Chance wasn't just handsome either; he was good on a horse—very good on a horse. And off a horse? Well, the man had an easy, rather sultry swagger that set Adelaide's heart to hammering every time she witnessed it.

Adelaide continued to watch Chance, mesmerized by everything about him. The fact was, Adelaide couldn't tear her gaze away from the brown-haired, blue-eyed, sun-bronzed man. She felt her heart giddyap in her bosom when the cowboy unexpectedly glanced toward where she and Janie stood on the bottom fence rung watching, touched the brim of his hat, and nodded in a silent hello. Although she couldn't truly hear his friendly greeting for the distance between them, her memory told her exactly how Chance Flannery's low, wildly affecting, Irish-accented voice sounded, and the knowledge caused goose bumps to ripple over her arms.

"Good gravy, Adelaide Plume!" Janie giggled. "I half expect yer tongue to slip outta yer mouth and start to drippin' drool!"

"Oh, you do not, Jane Higginson," Adelaide countered. "Besides, yer the one whose eyes are bulgin' out like a mouse in a spring-loaded bar trap. So don't go scoldin' me for admirin' nature's beauty over yonder."

Stepping up on the fence rung to stand next to his sister, Harvey Plume teased, "Oh, for cryin' out loud, girls. Ain't you two too proud and proper to be moonin' over cowboys?"

"We ain't moonin' over cowboys," Adelaide argued. "We're just admirin' that new cowhand's skill with a horse while he's cuttin' out ol' Mr. Worden's stock."

Harvey was handsome himself—tall, with light brown hair and green eyes. Unfortunately, he was well aware of the fact, and it lent him to owning a little too much self-confidence most of the time.

"Yeah, and I'm just as righteous as a preacher's wife," Harvey chuckled. He cocked his head to one side, seemed to study Chance Flannery himself for moment, and then remarked, "Still, I s'ppose if I was a silly schoolgirl, I'd think Chance was good-lookin' enough too. 'Specially for an Irishman." Harvey hopped over the fence then, adding over his shoulder, "But you two might want to roll your tongues back up into yer mouths before the fish start bitin'."

Adelaide frowned and grumbled, "Harvey's as welcome to me as a skunk at a Sunday lawn party. We ain't silly schoolgirls. Why, we've been outta school near to two years now."

"Dang right we have," Janie agreed. Still, in the next breath, she exhaled a sigh of longing. "That Harvey sure is a handsome skunk though. I'd up and marry him if he asked me."

Adelaide rolled her eyes, shaking her head. "Oh, I know you would," she giggled. Truth was, Janie Higginson had been sweet on Adelaide's brother Harvey for nigh unto a decade. But with Harvey thinking Janie was still a silly schoolgirl, Adelaide feared Harvey would never take serious notice of her friend. And she worried Janie would never get on over the fence about her oldest brother.

She studied Janie for a moment—wondering how on earth Harvey had managed *not* to notice Janie. After all, everyone knew Janie Higginson was the prettiest girl in town. Her golden hair and deep brown eyes were striking, to say the least. And she was kind, as well. Everything a good man ought to be lured in by.

"I don't know why ya can't just fall in love with Fordy," Adelaide remarked. "He's so much nicer than Harvey ever was." And it was true. Adelaide's other older brother, Ford, might not be as tall as Harvey was, but he was just as good-looking—if not better looking—as well as being a kinder, more courteous sort of man than Harvey.

Janie shrugged. "I tried once," she offered. "Remember? Two summers back? I spent all summer tryin' to change horses from Harvey to Fordy...but I just couldn't do it." She sighed a winsome sigh. "I guess the heart just wants who it wants, hmm?"

"I guess so," Adelaide admitted. She watched the new cowboy for a quiet moment, figuring there were most likely other daughters and granddaughters of other ranchers who had spent plenty of time daydreaming over him—wishing for a miracle that would win his heart. "Well, I guess if Harvey the Skunk thinks *you're* still a silly little girl and too young for him to really take notice of…then Chance Flannery's gonna think that about me too."

"It's the sad, sad truth," Janie sighed in disappointed agreement.

"Yes, indeedy," Adelaide confirmed, feeling less chipper than she had a few minutes before.

With one last lingering gaze at the ranch's new cowhand, Adelaide hopped off the fence rung. "I suppose it's time I got somethin' done…else Daddy will have my hide."

"Me too," Janie relented, stepping down with an exhale of disappointment. "Mama's wantin' me to get a coupla pies baked today, so I best get on home."

"I'll see you tomorrow then," Adelaide promised, hugging her friend.

"All right," Janie said, returning the friendly embrace.

Adelaide watched Janie mount her bay horse, Millie, and start toward home.

"Bye now," Janie called over her shoulder as she waved.

"Bye-bye," Adelaide chirped, returning the gesture. She felt a bit disheartened—just as she always did when she was left with no one but menfolk for company. Adelaide's mama had died giving birth to her, her grandma had died when Adelaide was just twelve, and her older brothers hadn't married yet to give her a sister-in-law or two. But the men in her family had stepped in and raised her with more love and attention than she figured most girls got, and she loved being with her daddy, brothers, and Pop.

Still, she did long to have an older woman around to talk to—to help her with improving her stitching and knitting, help her lace up her corsets and fix up her hair. She figured even having a good father, brothers, and grandfather couldn't completely compensate for not having a mother, grandma, aunt, or big sister nearby.

Adelaide's spirits didn't completely plummet, however, for just then she heard the familiar clanking of a big brass bell behind her. Smiling, she turned to see her steer, Roger, moseying toward her. His long horns dipped back and forth as he approached, and the clank, clank, clank rhythm of his bell made Adelaide's heart feel lighter once more.

"Roger!" she greeted with glee. "Where have you been all mornin', sugar plum?"

The nearly four-year-old, dark-red-and-white-marked longhorn steer ambling toward Adelaide picked up his pace as she motioned for him to come closer to her. Adelaide smiled as he bawled at her in glad anticipation. In a moment, his awkward run had closed the distance between them, and Adelaide hugged his thick, warm neck.

"There's my little Roger," Adelaide cooed as she stroked the steer softly on the forehead. "My! Aren't your horns bright and shiny this mornin'! I think they've grown a foot since yesterday, sweetheart!"

Roger snorted and nuzzled Adelaide with his wet nose.

"Ain't it a daisy of a day, Roger?" she asked the steer. "Look at that sky! Just look at it! Sun shinin' bright, and the breeze ain't too cool. I 'xpect we oughtta have ourselves a ride out to the old oak today. The weather's gonna turn any time now, and then we'll be in the barn more often than not. What do you say?"

Again Roger nuzzled Adelaide with his nose in obvious approval. Adelaide wiped at the moist spot his wet nose left on her sleeve. Oh, she didn't mind it much. She figured a little bovine mucus here and there was a small price to pay for the heartfelt affection she and Roger shared.

"Yep! I thought you'd agree," she giggled.

Using the second rung of the fence to boost herself, Adelaide hoisted herself up onto Roger's broad back.

"Giddyap there, darlin'," she urged him. "The sun doesn't wait on anybody."

Chance Flannery paused, his attention entirely engaged by the sight of the boss's granddaughter hoisting herself up onto the back of a big red-and-white longhorn steer. He watched, quirking one eyebrow with curiosity as the girl settled herself astride the animal's broad back, careless of showing her petticoats and stockinged legs from the knees down. She leaned forward, appearing to say something to the steer, and then clicked her tongue, setting it to walking on. In truth, he was a bit fascinated that such a young girl was riding away on the back of a longhorn.

"Yep," Harvey Plume began, reining up beside Chance. "That'd be my little sister, Adelaide. She's a bit odd...like a fine lady swappin' her moles for the mange."

"Did she break the thing for ridin' by herself then?" Chance asked, wishing his accent weren't so obvious. Most folks weren't bothered by Irishmen these days, but there were plenty who still frowned when they heard it. Yet the Plumes didn't seem to mind, and Chance was glad.

"Broke him, rides him, you name it," Harvey chuckled. "It ain't strange at all to be out ridin' and come across ol' Roger sprawled out under a tree with Addy fast asleep in the grass next to him, the two of 'em dreamin' about who knows what."

"Yar funnin' with me, ya are," Chance asked, grinning with amused doubt.

But Harvey shook his head. "Indeed not. Ol' Roger there was injured somethin' fierce when he was a calf. He got loose durin' brandin', ran through a barbed fence, and sliced hisself up miserable. We were able to stitch most of his wounds good enough…all but his scrotum. It was near to shredded, and Daddy had to castrate him. None of us believed he would make it through that first night. But Addy spent a week sleepin' with him out in the barn, and by the time Roger was all healed up, he was followin' her around like a puppy." Harvey laughed, adding, "And Roger ain't the only one. Last spring she saved a flock of little ducklings after their mama had been killed by a fox. And let me tell you, it was a sight to see! There they'd go, Adelaide walkin' along, seven little ducklings waddlin' along after her, and ol' Roger and his one-ton self a-moseyin' along after *them*. Damn steer thinks he's a dog, I reckon."

Chance chuckled as he tried to envision it—Pop Plume's granddaughter walking out with ducklings and a one-ton steer following after. It was sight he would've liked to see.

"Well, I've not seen the like in all me livin' days, that's far sure and far certain," he commented.

Harvey smiled, nodding, "Oh, believe me, Flannery…if you stay on long enough, you'll see my sister comin' up with far more peculiar goin's-on than a pet bull and mother-hennin' a flock of ducklin's! She does keep us entertained, I'll give her that."

"I should guess that she would then," Chance remarked.

Harvey turned his horse, ready to get back to work. But first he smiled and added, "She'll give ya a little competition on ridin' a horse too. Consider yerself warned, feller."

"She's that good on a harse, is she?" Chance inquired.

"Of course she is," Harvey assured with a smile. "I taught her everything I know." He chuckled then, adding, "Well, almost everything, that is."

Chance paused before reining back to cutting cattle. He watched Pop Plume's granddaughter riding off on her pet steer—thought how happy and free she looked with her long brown hair flouncing down over her back and shoulders. He heard her laugh as she said something to the animal, and the sound reminded him of a meadowlark song on a sunny summer morning.

He grinned, mumbling to his horse, "Move on then, Paddy. We got a big chore in front of us, we do."

It had only been two days since Chance had arrived in town hoping to find a ranch to winter on—only two days since Pop Plume had agreed to take him on. And yet he knew he'd struck gold already. The ranch was big but not too big, and Chance had enjoyed cowboying longhorns once before. There seemed to be plenty of work to keep the cowboys laboring for the Plumes busy for the long hours of the day but not so much that it couldn't be finished before dusk. The bunkhouse was sturdy and warm with plenty of room for a man to breathe his own air without having to endure the stench of some other cowboy's dirty feet.

Then there was Pop (Sam) Plume, his son, Mr. Dean Plume, and his grandsons, Harvey and Ford. They worked as hard as the cowboys it seemed, never complaining and never with an attitude of arrogance. Well, not as far as two days' working with them had proven anyway. All in all, Chance was already hoping he could sign on for good with the Plumes' longhorn ranch come spring. He was getting weary of looking for good ranchers to work for. He knew the big ranches were pushing the smaller ranchers to the side; all over the country it was true. Still, Chance was hoping he could cowboy for a few more years—until he had more money to his name and was a bit more worn out from it.

"Yer lettin' that little one run ya around a bit too much there, Fordy!" Chance heard Harvey holler.

"Oh, you mind yer own there, big brother," Fordy hollered as he headed for a quick little maverick that had slipped him. "If you'da fixed that fence the way Daddy told you, we wouldn't be cuttin' Worden's stock out in the first place."

Chance grinned, amused by the Plume brothers' banter. Yes, he knew he'd gotten lucky riding into town when he did. If his first two days were anything to measure it by, he ought to have a comfortable, as well as entertaining, winter.

Glancing back over his shoulder, he watched the longhorn steer and its girl rider amble away. "Could be a right entertain' winter, it could," he mumbled, grinning to himself. Silently he hoped some little nest of new ducklings would find themselves in need of another sort of mother come spring.

CHAPTER TWO

As the fire in the parlor hearth crackled with comforting warmth, Adelaide pulled the thread tight, securing the second yellow French knot at the center of the flower she'd been embroidering. She and Janie had decided to spend the cold, cloudy afternoon tucked away in Adelaide's parlor, finishing the items they were each donating to the Christmas bazaar. Oh, they had near to a week to finish, but the gloomy weather made indoor activities the best of choices. Drab, gray clouds hung low, veiling the warmth and bright countenance of the sun, yet without any threat or promise of rain. And thus it was the perfect sort of day for sitting near a glowing fire, enjoying the company of a bosom friend. And as they sat together—Adelaide embellishing a pillowcase with embroidery and Janie working at tatting the edge of a dishtowel—they conversed, as they often did, about their deepest secrets.

"I just can't seem to think about anything else," Adelaide admitted, beginning the third French knot of the embroidered flower's center. She sighed, continuing, "It all makes me feel…well, unhappy sometimes." She paused, shrugged, and then added, "If I'm bein' honest, it makes me feel unhappy *most* of the time."

"That's 'cause yer in love with him," Janie nonchalantly stated.

"What?" Adelaide exclaimed with a giggle. She glanced over to her friend, quickly admiring Janie—her flaxen hair pulled up into a perfect coiffure that gave her the appearance of being older than her near eighteen years. Shaking her head with amusement, Adelaide said, "Oh, that's nonsense. But you do know how to make me laugh, Janie, that's for sure and for certain."

Janie giggled, repeating, "'For sure and for certain,' is it?" in a contrived Irish brogue. "Ya know yer even startin' to sound like Chance, don't ya?"

Adelaide rolled her eyes with feigning indifference, but Janie continued, "And I'm not tryin' to make ya laugh, Adelaide," her gaze fixed on the intricate tatting at hand. "I'm serious as an ol' barn owl. You think about Chance all the time and feel unhappy when ya do because yer in love with him. Or in the least of it, ya know yer *gonna* fall in love with him."

Adelaide's smile faded, and her heart began to blister with a dull, dismal ache. Oh, she already knew she was sweet on Chance Flannery; she'd known that since the day he'd started cowboying on the ranch two months before. Simply thinking on Chance, watching him saunter toward his horse or the bunkhouse, talking with him— well, it had all been fun at first, made her cheerful, made her feel downright giddy. The very fact that Chance was walking over the same dirt and breathing the same air she was had kept Adelaide's heart hammering and made every day more wonderful—at least for the first month.

Nevertheless, in the recent weeks, Adelaide had begun to feel quite differently whenever she saw or thought about Chance. She'd begun to resent that her time in his company was so limited. Instead of feeling breathless and delighted by the smallest acknowledgements from him—instead of nearly swooning with bliss when his sky-blue gaze met the green of her own—Adelaide had begun to almost dread their interactions. For every time her heart would leap with joy because of some kind word or friendly smile offered to her by the handsome Irish cowboy, it would plummet to near despairing once the moment with him had ended.

The truth of it was, Adelaide knew what Janie was saying was true—absolutely true. As ridiculous as it was—as hopeless as it was—Adelaide knew that somewhere along the way, she'd gone from being sweet on Chance to falling in love with him. Still, it wasn't an easy matter for Adelaide to admit—even to herself. Especially now that Janie had rung the stake of truth with an iron horseshoe of fact out loud.

"And how do you know so much about it then?" Adelaide grumbled somewhat defensively.

"Because you've only been fallin' in love with Chance Flannery for two months...and I've been fallin' in love with Harvey for almost ten years, that's how," Janie kindly reminded.

Adelaide felt the heat of fresh humble pie rise to her cheeks. Janie was right. Adelaide's dearest friend had been carrying a torch for Adelaide's eldest brother for almost as long as Adelaide could remember.

"You're right, Janie," Adelaide apologized. "I don't know why I even go on about it all to you. It's downright selfish of me, and I'm so sorry."

Janie shrugged, pausing in her own work to look up to Adelaide and offer her a compassionate smile. "You know I want ya to talk it over with me. Heaven knows bein' able to talk over my *own* feelin's about Harvey with you is the only thing that has kept me out of the lunatic asylum these past coupla years. I only wish *one* of us wasn't so miserable and brokenhearted for pinin' away over some dang

13

man." Janie sighed with discouragement and returned her attention to her tatting. "It probably doesn't help things a whole lot that Chance gets along so awful well with yer brothers," Janie offered. " 'Cause bein' that Harvey obviously thinks the two of us are so young we oughta still be wearin' our hair in plaits, it surely must spill over onto the way Chance sees you."

Adelaide smoothed the long plait of her hair hanging over her left shoulder. At least it was one plait and not two. Surely one plait gave her the look of being a young woman of seventeen instead of a child. At least, she hoped it did. Still, she added her own sigh of disheartenment to the conversation. "And it certainly adds insult to injury that Harvey the Skunk is always sendin' Chance out to fetch me for somethin'." She growled a little, tossing her pillowcase and thread to the nearby sofa. "I swear! I could not believe it yesterday when Harvey sent him to fetch me for supper. Supper that *I* was cookin', by the way…supper that I knew would be ready when it was ready. But Harvey the Skunk sent Chance out to fetch me *again*…and Chance came into the barn and found me readin' out loud to Roger! I thought I was gonna curl up and die! I could wring Harvey's scrawny neck for that one."

Janie tried to stifle her giggle but failed, and Adelaide smoothed her apron and then tucked a loose strand of acorn hair behind her right ear in an effort to feel, if not appear, unrattled.

"What were ya readin'?" Janie asked, albeit with compassion. Adelaide knew Janie was trying to distract her from the fact Chance had found her reading out loud to her pet bovine. And she adored her all the more for it.

Adelaide rolled her eyes again, this time with embarrassment. "*The Picture of Dorian Gray*," she admitted in a whisper.

Janie gasped, looking to Adelaide with one hand pressed to her bosom in surprise. "You read *The Picture of Dorian Gray*? You read it to Roger...*out loud*?" she asked in aghast astonishment.

"Yes," Adelaide admitted, blushing with shame.

"I thought yer Daddy told you not to read that book!" Janie exclaimed, glancing about as if to ensure their privacy was complete.

"He did," Adelaide answered as guilt rose in her. "But I figured if I read it aloud to Roger...maybe it wouldn't be all that bad a thing."

"And?" Janie prodded.

Blushing with humiliation, Adelaide admitted, "It was worse readin' it aloud."

"Did...did Chance know exactly what ya were readin' to Roger?" Janie inquired, her eyes wide with anticipation.

"Oh, good gravy, I hope not!" Adelaide breathed with worry. "And I hope he hadn't been standin' outside the stall too awful long before he spoke to me...'cause I was readin' the most scandalous part of the book to Roger the very moment before he entered." Adelaide shook her head with disappointment in herself. "And Daddy was right; that is a book I should not have read." She felt tears well in her eyes, adding, "And I'm sure I've entirely corrupted poor Roger's innocent little soul! And to think what Chance Flannery must think of me...havin' found me readin' such mud."

Janie grinned, put down her tatting, and moved to sit next to Adelaide on the parlor sofa.

Placing comforting hands over Adelaide's, which were wringing in her lap, she soothed, "Oh, Roger is just fine, Addy. He probably doesn't understand more than a hundred words anyway. And as for Chance...ya don't know for certain that he heard exactly *what* ya were readin'." Janie shook her head, frowning a little, "I could turn

Harvey over my knee for always makin' sure Chance finds you in some awkward situation."

"He does it 'cause he's a skunk," Adelaide mumbled, taking her handkerchief from her apron pocket and dabbing away the moisture at the corner of her eyes. "And ya see this, Janie? See how flustered Chance Flannery has me? I swear I start weepin' here and there over things like this for no reason at all."

"And I'm tellin' ya the truth when I say that I know how yer feelin'," Janie reassured. She seemed pensive for a time, staring out through the big picture window of the parlor. Janie exhaled a heavy sigh and was quiet, continuing to gaze out the window.

Adelaide dabbed at her tears and listened to the crackle and pop of the warm fire, secretly wishing she had a mother to teach her how to pull her hair up the way Janie did. She was certain that if she could begin to wear her hair smoothly pulled up instead of in one long plait, everyone in all the world would see her as the woman she was—or at least was becoming—and not perceive her as a child any longer. Yet each time Adelaide had tried to coif her hair up on her own, it ended up looking like nothing more than a hastily constructed bird nest.

All at once, Janie looked to Adelaide and quite firmly stated, "Well, maybe it's time we made these men see that we are *not* little girls anymore—that we're full-grown women…women to be reckoned with…women to take notice of."

It took less than one tick of the Westminster chime clock on the mantel for Adelaide to realize what Janie was thinking and agree with wholehearted and determined exuberance. "Maybe it is indeed. After all, we are women! Women old enough to be courted—"

"Old enough to marry!" Janie interrupted resolutely. "After all, how old was yer mama when she married yer daddy?"

"Seventeen," Adelaide answered with a firm nod. "And six months younger than I am right this minute…'cause I'll be eighteen in three months and Mama was only three months into seventeen when she married Daddy."

"Dang right!" Janie confirmed. "And my mama was still sixteen when she married my daddy, and I'll be eighteen next month. So there ya have it! We *are* old enough to be recognized as women," Janie nodded, reassuring herself and Adelaide.

"Well, to be quite honest, Janie," Adelaide began, "*you* already look eighteen. Nineteen even. You've got yer hair all pulled up nice and pretty, and this new green dress you're wearin'…" Adelaide paused, reaching out and gently tugging the sleeve of Janie's new forest-green day dress. "On the other hand, I couldn't pull my hair up nicely and make it stay if my life depended on it."

"Oh, nonsense!" Janie argued. "I can show ya how to fix up yer hair. And you're already workin' on a new dress, that pretty red you're finishin' up for the Christmas bazaar and dance next week." Janie paused a moment, her eyes glinting with mischief. "And why don't we make *that* the time and place that we show this town and every cowboy in it that we *are* eligible women instead of just silly schoolgirls, hmm?"

Adelaide smiled as excitement and hope leapt in her bosom. "Hmmm…that does sound intriguin', my dear Miss Higginson." Adelaide gazed out through the parlor window and into the gray sky. "I can just imagine it—you and I enterin' the big barn wearin' new evenin' dresses, our hair piled high on our heads. We'll be lookin' just like two true ladies." She winked at Janie, "Two grown-up, refined ladies, of course."

"Of course," Janie agreed with a giggle.

As the back kitchen door burst open—as Adelaide's daddy and grandpa entered the kitchen, both exclaiming that the two apple pies cooling on the counter smelled like heaven itself, Adelaide whispered to Janie, "We'll have to talk more about this tomorrow. The hands will be comin' in for supper soon."

Janie nodded and giggled softly. "Well, bein' that yer daddy has asked you to feed the hands one good supper a week so they don't have to eat the same old beans and bacon they make every night...at least we can be sure Chance knows what a good cook you are!"

"At least there's that," Adelaide giggled.

"Is supper almost ready, Addy?" Pop hollered from the kitchen. "I swear I'm so hungry I could eat a bear tonight!"

"Yes, sir, Pop!" Adelaide assured him. "As soon as everyone is seated at the table, we'll get started." She could hear her brothers and the other cowboys entering the kitchen—their boots clomping across the kitchen floor, the screech of legs as chairs were slid to the large table.

"I best be gettin' home," Janie sighed.

"You're more than welcome to stay for supper here, Janie," Adelaide offered.

"Oh, I know," Janie assured her, stuffing her tatting materials into the cloth bag she'd brought with her. "But I've got to get some more quilts on the beds this evenin'. Daddy says it's gonna be so cold, the milk cows will be givin' icicles in the mornin'."

"You want one of the boys to see ya home, Janie?" Adelaide's father asked, stepping into the parlor just then.

"Oh no, thank you, Mr. Plume," Janie assured Dean Plume as she pulled on her coat. "It's only two miles; you know that."

But Adelaide smiled, winking at Janie when her father's booming voice echoed as he called over his shoulder, "Fordy...see that Janie gets home all right. I don't like the look of them clouds out there."

"You bet," Fordy agreed without hesitation.

Janie's cheeks pinked up with embarrassment, and Adelaide winked at her, whispering, "Ya know my daddy worries over women ridin' out by themselves."

Janie nodded, still blushing. Adelaide knew darn well that the reason her daddy was having Fordy see Janie home instead of Harvey was because her daddy knew Fordy was a better choice to be sweet on than Harvey was—for any girl in town.

"Mr. Plume," Janie began as she followed Adelaide into the kitchen, "it really isn't necessary to have—"

"Like hell it ain't!" Adelaide's father interrupted with a chuckle. "My mama would take to rollin' over in her grave if I sent ya out in this menacin' weather on yer own, Janie. Ain't that right, Pop?"

"Damn right," Pop Plume affirmed with a nod.

"'Sides, Fordy don't mind at all," Dean continued. "'Specially since I'm sure there's an extra slice of pie waitin' for him when he gets back. Ain't that right, Fordy?"

"That's right," Fordy assured with a smile as he fetched his hat off the hat rack near the kitchen door. "It won't take me but a few minutes there and back, Janie. I'm glad to do it."

Still blushing, Janie nodded her thanks to Fordy. "Very well," she sighed, resolved to defeat. She giggled then, calling, "I'll race you to the hitchin' post *and* home, Fordy Plume!" as she hitched up her skirt and petticoat a bit and hurried past Fordy and out the door.

Fordy laughed as he plopped his hat on his head, scrambling to put his coat on as he followed.

Adelaide giggled and returned the mischievous wink her father gave her with an understanding one of her own. Dean Plume looked out for everybody—and that included seeing that young ladies kept the best company as well as had an escort home on a dreary evening.

Adelaide's pop was already seated on one end of the table when her daddy sat himself at the other. Harvey, Chance, and the other four cowboys—Ike, Earle, Boney Bob, and Cliff—took seats on each side of the table and folded their hands in preparation for the blessing on the food that would be given.

"Oh, here ya go, Addy," Harvey said as he slid over to sit in the chair perpendicular from her daddy's—the chair that was usually hers for supper. Gesturing to the now empty chair between him and Chance Flannery, Harvey suggested, "Go on and sit here. It'll take Fordy more than just a few minutes to see Janie home. Ya might as well have his seat."

"All right," Adelaide agreed, pasting on a false smile and willing herself not to blush, for she knew exactly what Harvey was doing: he was positioning her next to Chance on purpose. No doubt he had some malicious scheme working around in his head. But Adelaide wasn't about to let him know he'd rattled her. No indeed.

"Here, let me get that for ya," Harvey said, standing and pulling out the chair for Adelaide, as any gentleman should.

"Thank you," Adelaide said as she smoothed her skirt over her behind and began to sit down.

Boy, oh boy, did she hit the floor hard! Her fanny and tailbone stung with the force of meeting the floor instead of the chair's seat.

As Harvey whooped and hollered, amused with himself for pulling the chair back farther instead of gently sliding it under Adelaide's sitter as she sat, Adelaide gasped when she felt two strong hands around her waist. Simultaneously, she startled when the table shook with the force of her father's and grandpa's fists smashing down onto it in unison.

"Dammit, Harvey!" Dean Plume bellowed.

"Are ya all right there, lassy?" Chance asked as he pulled Adelaide to her feet, his warm, strong hands lingering at her waist to ensure she got her footing.

"Y-yes. Thank you, Ch-Chance," she managed, fighting back the stinging tears of pain and humiliation that were welling in her eyes.

"Ya be certain, lassy?" Chance asked, sounding unconvinced.

Venturing a glance at him—feeling lost in the beautiful blue of his sincerely concerned gaze, noting that his furrowed brows gave him an unnervingly intimidating presence—she answered, "I'm certain."

Chance's hands left her waist, and he took hold of the back of the chair Harvey had pulled out from under her. "Here y'are, Miss Adelaide," Chance said. "Let me be gettin' that far ya."

"Thank you," Adelaide said, barely managing to keep from bursting into tears. She managed to keep her tears at bay only with pure determination not to give Harvey the satisfaction.

Harvey—still standing, still chuckling over what he thought was a great prank—pulled out his own chair and began to sit down. Yet no sooner had he released the back of his chair and started his sitter's descent than Chance reached over, yanking the chair back and sending Harvey sprawling to the floor.

Ike, Earle, Boney Bob, and Cliff chuckled as Harvey stared up at Chance in astonishment—and then anger.

"Hey, boy," Harvey growled, "remember who ya work for."

"Oh, don't be worryin' yar cabbage head about that, jackass," Chance countered. "I work for Mr. Sam and Mr. Dean Plume, I do. And me own mother would skin me bloody if I were to allow a man to treat his own sister that way, she would. No matter if I worked for him or not."

"Yer pretty big for yer britches, Irishman," Harvey said, scowling as he rose to his feet.

"That's it!" Pop bellowed. "I swear, Harvey—if you didn't look so much like yer daddy, I'd think you weren't a Plume at all."

"Why, I'm downright embarrassed to admit that ya do look like me, boy," Dean grumbled. "You were not taught to treat women with such disrespect."

"I don't treat women with disrespect, Pa," Harvey argued. He looked to Adelaide then, grinning. "But Addy ain't no woman. She's just my sister."

Adelaide avoided looking at her father then, for she knew what was coming. Dean Plume was a peaceful man—unless a situation called for something other than peacefulness. And she knew that to her father and grandfather—well, Harvey had poked two big bears, and no doubt there would be hell to pay.

"Now I ain't gonna deny you supper, Harvey," Dean said, his face red with anger, "'cause I want a hard day's work outta you, and starvin' ya won't get me that. Furthermore, I want a hard *night's* work outta you too."

"What?" Harvey exclaimed. "Yer gonna make me prowl the fence lines tonight? I already done it two days ago. It ain't my turn."

Dean Plume was on his feet then. "Remember who *you* work for, boy!" he rumbled. "Now serve yerself up some stew, and head on out to the back porch. You ain't eatin' at my table tonight. Also, you apologize to yer sister! And you be sure you thank her for them victuals she spent all day cookin' up…else I'll change my mind and starve ya whether or not yer working the fence line 'til midnight!"

Adelaide looked up to Harvey, glaring at him with utter loathing in that moment.

Glaring down at her, Harvey grumbled, "I'm sorry, Addy. I shouldn'ta done that. I'm sorry."

"Get yer stew and head on out to the porch," Adelaide said, nodding in accepting his apology, albeit far less than sincerely.

Everyone watched in silence as Harvey took a plate from the stack sitting next to the massive pot of beef-and-vegetable stew sitting on the stovetop. Using the large ladle Adelaide had provided, he heaped his plate with steaming stew, snatched up a spoon and two slices of bread, and stormed out of the kitchen to the back porch.

Adelaide looked to her father as he took his seat. "I am so sorry, Addy," her father sighed. "I do not know where his bad behavior comes from. I'm so sorry. I can't believe that boy is pushin' twenty-three years old. He ain't got the maturity of a half-weaned pup."

"It's not yer fault, Daddy," Adelaide soothed, smiling lovingly at her handsome father. She noted how much Harvey really did look like her father—tall, handsome, green-eyed with brown hair. Her daddy was distinguishedly graying at the temples, and it only added to his good looks. On the other hand, his countenance was far more handsome than her oldest brother's, for Dean Plume was a hard-working, kind, compassionate, strong gentleman—and Harvey Plume was a skunk.

"And I want to thank you, Chance," her father added, nodding to Chance with approval.

"Far what, sir?" Chance inquired.

"For steppin' up and givin' Harvey what he was owed," Pop answered. "You sure ain't no gutless goat, boy. And I admire that."

Chance nodded his appreciation and then clasped his hands together, indicting he would rather the attention be removed from him and put back to the meal at hand.

"In fact, why don't you be the one to offer up thanks for supper tonight, there, Chance?" Dean asked.

"'Twould be me pleasure, it would, sir."

Chance gritted his teeth, trying to settle his temper before he addressed the Lord in thanking him for the good meal he was about to enjoy. He wondered for a moment how on earth he was going to manage to get through a blessing when he was so fired up—and without asking that somehow Harvey Plume get his rightful comeuppance for what he'd done to his little sister only moments before.

Chance liked cowboying for the Plumes—more than anybody he'd ever worked for. But Harvey Plume was a burr under his saddle for many reasons—his ill treatment of his sister being at the top of the list.

Still, Chance inhaled a deep breath and began, "Our most gracious Lard in Heaven…" Another deep breath, and he was calm enough—or so he hoped. "It's grateful we are, all of us…most grateful, indeed…for this bonny meal that the kind Miss Plume has prepared far us this evenin'. Thank ye far her kind hands in laborin' for the sake of us all…even feedin' her donkey of a brother who may not be as deservin' as some others. This humble thanks we give to thee, Lard…in the name of Christ our Savior, Amen."

Adelaide bit her lip to keep from giggling—for although it was obvious that Chance was as sincere as any somber preacher in his words, his reference to Harvey had not only caused a giggle in her throat but also sent her heart soaring with appreciation and welling admiration.

"Well said, boy…well said," Pop chuckled, standing from his seat and heading for the stewpot.

"Thank ya, sir," Chance accepted.

"Nice prayer," Ike said, smiling at Chance. Boney Bob, Earle, and Cliff nodded in agreement, chuckling under their breath.

Adelaide's smile broadened. She knew the other cowboys, including Fordy, liked Chance—liked him for his skill with a horse, his good-natured sense of humor, and his integrity. She'd heard them discussing it once when she'd been in the barn brushing Roger as they had been saddling up their horses. In Adelaide's estimation, Chance was pure gold when it came to men. And his trilling Rs and Irish accent only added to his charisma.

"Here ya go, Addy darling," Pop said, sliding a plate of stew onto the table in front of Adelaide. He handed her a spoon and a slice of bread, adding, "I sure do like these suppers when the boys are all together. Thank ya for the fixin's, honey."

"You're welcome, Pop," Addy said, musing for a moment on how handsome all the men in her family were—on what good men they were. She figured that once Harvey grew up a bit more, even he'd be a good man and deserving of the Plume men's attractiveness of face and form.

Never would any man in all the world be as handsome, as charming, and as wonderful as Chance Flannery, however. Adelaide knew that as certain as she knew the sky was blue above the gray clouds that were starting to dissipate. If Harvey was the dismal gloom in a day, Chance was the resplendent sunshine that chased it away.

CHAPTER THREE

"There we go," Adelaide cooed, stroking Roger's forehead. "The clouds have cleared, but bein' that I could see our breath while we were out walkin', it's gonna be a cold night. But that's why you have your own cozy stall right here in the barn, darlin'…" She planted one last kiss on Roger's velvety head. "'Cause Daddy knows I'd never get a wink of sleep if I had to worry about you freezin' at night." One more loving pat on Roger's back and Adelaide left his stall, closing the half-door behind her and making sure the latch was secure.

"Night-night, sweetheart," she called, wrapping her coat more tightly around her body. Adelaide sighed with contentment in knowing her beloved pet steer would be safe and warm. She offered a silent prayer of thanks for the fact that her daddy had allowed her and Fordy to combine two barn stalls into one, once Roger had grown so big that the breadth of his horns would no longer allow him to be comfortable in just a regular stall. Dean Plume was a good man and a caring father—and Adelaide was grateful for it.

Stepping out of the barn and into the cold quiet of night, Adelaide secured the barn door and then turned, gazing up into the dark, indigo firmament. As much as Adelaide disliked the long, cold months of winter, she loved winter's night sky. When it was clear of storms and clouds, the stars in the heavens winked with a brilliance unmatched by any other starry night of the year. Oh, it was true that Adelaide loved the night sky, the stars, and the moonlight any time of the year. But it was the winter's night sky that fascinated her most. On nights such as this one, it seemed the stars twinkled with more vigor and the moonlight's gossamer rays of sterling shone more lustrous, as well. The *Farmers' Almanac* promised the moon would be full and radiant in all its glory at Christmas, and Adelaide could think of no more wonderful a gift than a full moon on Christmas Eve.

Secretly, she loved the moon for reasons not even her family knew. Ever since she was a little girl—ever since the day her grandmother had promised her that her mother was watching over her from heaven and that the moon was a peephole through which those who had traveled beyond to eternity could watch over their loved ones—Adelaide had loved the moon. Naturally, as she grew older, she realized that the moon wasn't truly a peephole from heaven. Nonetheless, the notion that her mother and her grandmother were in heaven looking down from the same moon that Adelaide was gazing up at made her feel more connected to them. Whenever she felt most alone or frightened, Adelaide would sit out under the night sky, admiring the stars and talking to her mother and grandmother while staring up at the heavenly peephole that was the moon. It was calming—comforting—and she often felt a quiet peacefulness wash over her that she knew could only be explained as consolation sent from heaven—from those she knew and loved there.

Adelaide decided to enjoy the night sky for a few moments longer and soon settled herself on one of the old logs surrounding the firepit nearby. Earlier, the cowboys had built a fire around which they could warm themselves between chores and managing the herd. But no calves were being branded, of course; no cowboys were using the firepit to cook their beans and bacon. After all, the men had eaten in the house with Adelaide and her family that evening. Therefore, she was alone with the smoldering red and orange embers of a dying fire to warm her and a sky too beautiful not to appreciate. She wrapped her knitted scarf over her head and around her neck, tucking it into her coat for added warmth, exhaling a sigh of gratification.

She inhaled deeply, savoring the becalming aroma of burning cedar wood mingled with cool, fresh air, and thought to herself that there was no more comforting a fragrance in all the world.

And yet the memory of the mean-spirited antics of her brother, Harvey the Skunk, at supper earlier in the evening intruded on Adelaide's contentment. Truth was, her tailbone still hurt. She wondered how long it would ache from her fall to the floor when Harvey had pulled her chair out from under her. Adelaide felt her brows pucker in a frown as she thought on the incident. Still, she shook her head a little, determined she would enjoy the moonlight and not think about Harvey. And indeed, warmth began simmering in her heart as she thought of Chance helping her to her feet— thought of the strength of his hands at her waist and the way he'd given Harvey back what he had put out. It had been a truly romantic gesture in Adelaide's estimation. Oh, certainly she knew Chance was simply being a gentleman and trying to assist a female in distress. But it caused butterflies to begin flapping in her stomach all the same.

She closed her eyes for a moment and thought of Chance's voice—tried to recall exactly how his voice sounded when he'd called her "lassy," inquiring of her well-being. She loved his accent, especially when he addressed her as "lassy," as he had done on several occasions, instead of Miss Adelaide. Even when he'd entered the barn the day before at Harvey's prodding to find her reading *The Picture of Dorian Gray*—even in those horrid moments of humiliation, her heart had nearly beat itself out of her bosom with delight when Chance had asked, "I'm sorry for the intrusion, I am, lassy...but yar eldest brother is wantin' ya for some reason, he is."

For all the embarrassment of Chance finding her lying in the straw next to Roger and reading such a scandalous, unscrupulous book, his addressing her as "lassy" had nearly sent her into a swoon spurred by bliss.

"Aye, lassy, yar out late ya are...and in such cold weather."

For a brief moment, her eyes still closed, Adelaide thought she'd imagined Chance's speaking to her—imagined his bewitching Irish brogue. Quickly, however, she realized that the nearly imperceptible shift of the log she was sitting on meant someone had settled down next to her. Opening her eyes, she found that she had not conjured up the savory sound of his voice, for Chance was indeed sitting on the log next to her—smiling at her.

"Are ya not cold, lass? Seems to me yar nose might go numb in this chilly air," Chance offered, his mesmerizing gaze affixed to hers.

The lure of his gaze and delicious lilt of his intonation caused a giggle of delight to bubble up in her throat and into her mouth. Adelaide could feel the heat of blushing on her cheeks and hoped that Chance would think it was simply the cold weather pinking them up.

"No...not yet anyway," she managed, returning his smile. She was always so delightfully jittery whenever Chance was looking at her. To Adelaide, it always felt as if the blue of his eyes could see right into her very soul and know her thoughts—her deepest desires and secrets.

"I-I love the moonlight," she stammered, "and the stars…especially in winter."

At last Chance's attention left her face, and he looked heavenward. "Aye. 'Tis the winter's night sky seems much more clear and fresh…the stars more brilliant, it does."

Adelaide's reprieve from the bewitching vitality of his blue-eyed attention was brief, however. For he returned his considerations to her face once more—as if he found her more interesting to look at than the shimmering stars and delicate moonlight.

"It's glad I am to find ya here," Chance began, "for I wanted to be sure and certain that ya know how much I appreciated that fine meal ya prepared for us this evenin'. 'Twas the best beef-and-vegetable stew I've had in all me life, it was."

Adelaide's blush burned warmer as she properly accepted his compliment. "Oh, I'm so very glad you enjoyed it." Her heart was hammering so hard in her bosom it was causing her ears to ring!

"And that's not just flattery, lass," Chance added. "It truly was the best stew of me life." He paused, his brow puckering a moment. He appeared pensive for just an instant and then smiled again and said, "Well, truth be told…that chicken-and-vegetable stew ya stirred up week before last—the one with the sage and thyme biscuits on top—maybe *that* was the best stew of me life." He winked at her, proposing, "Though I might need to be tastin' them both next to one another to make a decision of certainty. Yet either one—the beef or the chicken—ahhh! I could die a happy man with one or the other as me last meal, I could."

"Well, although I'm confident that yer exaggeratin', Mr. Flannery, I'll say thank you again and assure you that I'll continue to slop up supper for ya once a week for as long as you'd like me to."

He chuckled, and the deep, warm sound caused goose bumps to ripple over Adelaide's arms and neck.

"Thank ye, lass," he said. "But I would think you'd have taken to callin' me Chance after all these weeks. Far I'd much prefer it if ya would. Mr. Flannery…it makes me feel like an old man, and I'm far and away from an old man, I hope, don't ya think?"

"Oh yes…far from an old man," Adelaide sighed, gazing at him and wishing with all she was that he would see her as more than Harvey the Skunk's little sister. Realizing she'd sighed her answer with obvious admiration and was probably staring at him like a love-struck pup, Adelaide straightened her posture, looked to the glowing embers in the firepit, and asked, "Why does Daddy have you all ridin' the fence lines during the night? Not that I don't think Harvey deserves to ride the fence lines…but am I to understand you men are ridin' the fence lines all night, every night?"

Chance felt his smile fade—looked to the warm embers winking in the firepit. He had not been prepared for Adelaide Plume to ask him the reason her father and grandfather had put the men to watching over the herd through the night by keeping the fence lines secure. His instincts as a man told him to protect the boss's daughter—let her drift to sleep that night on the wings of feeling secure and safe. Still, Chance didn't believe in lying either. For one thing, it was a sin. For another, he'd never seen any good come from telling lies.

Naturally, he could answer that it wasn't his place to tell her—that she should ask her father or grandfather, or even Harvey or Fordy. Still, sending her off to someone else for an answer might make the situation seem worse and more frightening than it needed to.

"Um…a few head of cattle have come up missin' these past two weeks, they have," he began. "And not just from the Plume ranch…but from Mr. Worden's place, as well."

He looked to Adelaide to see her pretty brow pucker with concern. Ah, but she was a bonny lass! Her bright green eyes reminded him of the plush green of Ireland's pastures—her soft brown hair of the aromatic coffee his grandmother used to brew for his grandfather on cool, misty mornings.

"Rustlers?" Adelaide asked. "Do Daddy and Pop think there are rustlers 'round here?"

Chance quirked one eyebrow and shrugged. "Not a body has seen any," he explained. "But there's no sign of the missin' cattle…none. We tracked hoof prints—harses with riders and herdin' a few head—all the way to the river. But the traces ended there, and yar father thinks they took them downstream, he does. But beyond knowin' they were taken, we found nothin'."

"Well, have Pop and Daddy…have they told the sheriff?" she asked, obviously disturbed—and angered. "Surely Sheriff Abel can do something!"

Chance nodded, reaching out and placing a hand on the girl's forearm in an effort to keep her calm.

"The sheriff knows, he does," he assured her. "But until someone finds a rustler or the missin' cattle or a better way to track them…well, yar father is havin' us ride the fence lines. He's hopin' that our presence during the day and all night will discourage whoever is takin' the cattle and cause them to move on, he is. And I think they will." Unsure as to how to further reassure her, Chance put his arm around her slight shoulders and patted her shoulder.

"So don't ya be worryin', lass," he added. "We'll make certain the cattle are protected and that yar kept safe, we will." He saw her glance beyond him to the barn, her frown deepening. "As well as those loved ones in the barn," he added, knowing she was worried about her steer.

The thought of Adelaide Plume and her pet steer caused amusement to rise in Chance, and he hoped the girl didn't take offense if she should see the merriment in his eyes. She was a very pretty thing, with a loving heart the like Chance had never seen before. He found it most endearing. After all, he couldn't imagine there were many young women in the world that had so attached themselves to a two-ton steer the way she had. The wondering thought traveled through his mind (as it often had since he'd begun working for the Plumes)—*How old is Adelaide Plume exactly? Is she old enough for a man to court her?* It seemed that if she were, the suitors would be lined up at Dean Plume's door begging the hand of his daughter. And yet she yet wore her hair in a plait—or even very often let it hang free. Thus, Chance didn't know whether to shame himself for thinking she was the prettiest little lass he'd ever seen or to allow himself to tease and flirt with her—to treat her like a young woman instead of a schoolgirl on the cusp of womanhood.

He pushed his musings to the back of his mind then, and in an effort to distract her from the threat of rustlers, Chance offered, "Now, between me and ye…how are we goin' to get that eldest brother of yars to keep off yar tail, hmmm?"

Chance was glad when Adelaide's countenance changed from that of worry to irritation.

"Oh, Harvey is a cloud on my every horizon," she groaned. "I can put up with his tryin' to humiliate and embarrass me all the dang time. But when he pulled that chair out from under me this evenin'…"

Chance frowned as she reached around to rub her tailbone.

"Well, it hurt like the devil! Still hurts, for that matter," she sighed. Then she looked to him, her eyes sparkling as she gazed at him a moment. "And that reminds me, thank you again for standin' up for me, Mr…. Chance. It meant the world to me… and…and…thank you."

Chance smiled at her as his arm left her shoulders. Her heart was still pounding from his kind gestures, and she wished she hadn't been wearing a coat—for she knew it would've been pure bliss to have felt his touch with less padding as an impediment.

"It was me pleasure, lass. He's not a very kind brother to ye at times. I think ya should stand up to him a bit more than ya do. Yar a lady, after all, and ya deserve to be treated as such…even by yar brother."

Adelaide nodded. Chance was right. Although her daddy, Fordy, and Pop had always come to her rescue or defense where Harvey was concerned—that is, if they knew he was up to no good on her behalf—she *was* a lady now, and she did deserve to be treated like one.

"You're right," she firmly stated. "I should stand up to him more. Even if it means I have to tell Daddy and get him in trouble, shouldn't I?"

Chance chuckled, "Oh, ya might not always have to tell on him to keep him in line. There're other ways to manage it, there are."

"Other ways?" Adelaide asked, perplexed. "What do ya mean?"

Chance winked at her. "Let me think on it a bit longer, lass. I'll conjure a way or two to give ya a foot up on yar brother, I will. Bur for now, there's a lot that can be accomplished by just not lettin' him know he's gettin' yar goat."

"How?"

"Well…like yesterday," Chance began. "When yar skunk of a brother sent me out to remind ye supper was simmerin'…do not let him know it embarrassed ye."

Adelaide's cheeks pinked. "But…but ya heard me readin' to Roger. It *was* embarrasin'. I'm just glad you didn't know what I was…"

When she paused too long, horrified that she's almost admitted she'd been reading scandalous literature to Roger, Chance leaned closer to her and whispered, "Ah, *The Picture of Dorian Gray*, it was. A dark tale of a twisted man. It quite intrigued me, it did. And I'm certain Roger has never had such an adventure."

Adelaide's eyes widened, and she asked in a whisper, "*You've* read *The Picture of Dorian Gray?*"

"Aye," Chance admitted. "We all have our secret moments of folly, now don't we? Our morbid curiosities."

Adelaide giggled. "The endin' *was* quite morbid, wasn't it?"

"Aye, 'twas most satisfyingly morbid," he agreed, smiling with understanding.

Still, as she thought of the book and the fact that she'd wished she'd never read it—especially out loud to Roger—Adelaide offered, "I hope you don't think too badly of me Mr.…um…Chance. I-I would never have read it if I'd known how scandalous it was and—"

"Ya don't be needin' to worry about judgment from me, lass," Chance heroically interrupted. "Me mother nearly skinned me alive when she found out I'd been reading *Huckleberry Finn* to me little brother," he revealed. "She said it would turn us both into naughty imps inclined toward mischief, far sure and far certain." He grinned, winked at her, and added, "And oh, merry imps of mischief we were indeed. But we were impish long before we read the works of Mr. Twain."

Adelaide giggled, delighted by the spark of mischief that had leapt to Chance's eyes as he spoke of his family.

"Pop says boys are born with mischief already in them," she offered.

"Snips and snails and puppy dog tails, as the poem goes, aye?" he chuckled. He frowned, pensive. "I have yet to larn what a 'snip' is."

"I read that the original poem was written as '*snigs* and snails and puppy dog tails'—and that a snig was a sort of eel or somethin' somewhere in England," Adelaide commented.

"Aye! *That* I can understand!" Chance exclaimed with a low laugh.

His smile broadened as he seemed to study Adelaide's face for a moment, and she blushed under his intense inspection.

"Ya're sendin' me to sleep with a lighter heart and a smile, lassy," Chance complimented. "Thank ye for that."

Adelaide blushed again and found she was so delighted she couldn't muster a verbal answer, and so she nodded.

"And don't ya be worryin' about them vanishin' cattle, all right?" he said, wagging an index finger at her. "None of us will be lettin' any more be lost."

"All right," she managed.

"Now," Chance began, "it's off to slumberin', I am...far the sun'll be up sooner than later, it will."

He stood and offered her a hand, in gesturing he thought she would be going in, as well. And although Adelaide had planned on sitting out under the moon and stars for a bit longer—planned on watching the fire embers die altogether—nothing in all the world was worth missing the opportunity to take Chance Flannery's hand when he offered it.

Therefore, taking his hand and giggling as he pulled her to her feet, Adelaide offered a quiet thank you before gazing up into his handsome face and saying, "Good night, Chance."

"Good night, lass," he said, his deep brogue scattering goose bumps over every inch of her body.

♥

Adelaide gazed out her bedroom window to the bright moon and stars in the midnight sky. As tired as she was, she knew it would be hours more before she would be able to fall asleep. The time she'd spent with Chance at the firepit earlier had left her in a cloud of euphoria, her heartbeat increasing every time she thought of his eyes and attention being fixated on her and her alone. The trilling Rs of his brogue echoed in her ears like a provocative whisper, and the mere memory of it caused her skin to warm.

And as she lay in bed—envisioning Chance's face and form, recalling his voice, kindness, understanding, compassion, and protective nature—Adelaide was determined that he *would* come to see her as more than Dean Plume's eccentric daughter or Harvey Plume's tormented little sister. When he saw her in her new red dress at the Christmas bazaar and dance the next week—when he saw her with her hair pulled up the way Janie wore hers and looking like a grown-up lady instead of out riding Roger with a windblown mop on her head and looking like a wild-haired ragamuffin schoolgirl—then surely Chance would see her differently.

"I'll make him see," she whispered to herself with rising hope. "I will."

Adelaide smiled, looking directly at the big silvery peephole in the night sky. "You watch me, Mama! You'll see, Grandma! One day soon, Chance Flannery will be askin' Daddy for permission to come courtin'. He will! You just wait and see!"

She imagined the moon darkened for a moment. And when it brightened again, Adelaide Plume was certain it had winked at her with approval and assurance that all would be as she had avowed it would be.

CHAPTER FOUR

"Be careful up there," Janie called from under the enormous oak.

"I'm always careful," Adelaide assured from the thick, sturdy branch she sat astride high above.

"It doesn't look to me like yer bein' careful, Addy!" Janie hollered as Adelaide stretched one arm farther out on the limb, trying to reach the massive nest of mistletoe. "I really do think we have enough!"

"We need as much as we can get, Janie," Adelaide reminded her friend. "*And* we want to make sure what we do have is just drippin' with berries, or else it won't last 'til the end of the night."

"Well, if yer determined to slather every frame of every door in the big barn with mistletoe, you best be sure you live long enough to stand under it with somebody, Adelaide Plume! You are givin' me the willies with how high up ya are!"

"Just…a…little…farther out…" Adelaide mumbled to herself as she scooted farther out on the limb. Finally, she reached the enormous clump of mistletoe she'd set her sights on. "There!" she laughed with triumph as she used the scissors, which she'd tied to her waist with a ribbon, to begin cutting bunches of the tree's parasite. "This one is just bustin' with berries, Janie!" she giggled.

"Everyone who attends the bazaar and dance tonight should be able to get a kiss and pluck a berry off!"

"I admire yer thoughtfulness, Addy. I do," Janie encouraged, still sounding unsettled, however. "But be careful!"

"Okay, here comes the first one," Adelaide called as she readied to drop the first cluster of mistletoe she'd cut away to Janie.

"I'm ready," Janie assured her.

Adelaide watched as Janie did indeed catch the mistletoe.

"I'll drop the rest down to you and then come down and help ya tie 'em up with ribbons," she explained. Giggling to herself, she added, "There's gonna be more mistletoe in the big barn than this town has ever seen."

Adelaide adored mistletoe! Oh, she knew it was a bad plant, really—that the old oak would probably die younger than it would have had the parasitic plant never found its way into its branches. Nevertheless, she loved the white-berried plant that was traditionally found hung over thresholds at Christmastime—loved it because of what it stood for: kissing!

When Adelaide was a little girl, her grandmother had told her all the histories of mistletoe and its traditions, as well as legends surrounding it—ancient peoples believing it to be a symbol of fertility, Romans hanging mistletoe in doorways to protect their homes with love and peace, and early Christians using it to ward off witches and demons. But Adelaide most adored the kissing traditions of the past one hundred years or so. Her grandmother had explained that a hundred years before, servants in England preserved the tradition of kissing under the mistletoe and in fact were the source of the tradition's popularity and the cause of its being spread throughout the world. There had even been a time when any man could kiss any woman while she was standing beneath the mistletoe and that bad luck would befall the woman if she refused. Furthermore, the belief was once held that an unmarried man and unmarried woman who kissed beneath mistletoe were bound to be eternal lovers and marry. But it was her grandmother's story of the tradition of a berry being plucked from a cluster of hanging mistletoe each time a couple kissed beneath it that found Adelaide willing to gather the most berry-laden clusters of the plant. A mistletoe cluster picked clean of berries by kissing couples rendered it useless to provide the privilege of kissing—a tradition that her grandmother herself had implemented at annual Christmas celebrations when she and Pop had first moved to town. To Adelaide, *that* was the legendary tradition of mistletoe she loved most.

Thus, as she cut and dropped cluster after cluster of mistletoe bursting with berries down to Janie, Adelaide's excitement rose. Janie hoped to be captured by Harvey under one of the mistletoe bouquets she and Adelaide would decorate with red ribbon and hang in every doorway in the town's big barn. But Adelaide had been daydreaming for days and days that perhaps, just perhaps, she might manage to find herself under the kissing plant at the very moment Chance Flannery was entering or leaving the barn that night.

"Last one!" Adelaide called as she dropped the final mistletoe cluster she'd cut.

"Thank heaven!" Janie sighed with relief. "Now shinny back down here before ya break yer neck!"

"All right, all right," Adelaide agreed. "I'm comin' down."

And yet she paused—for the huge nest of mistletoe was still bursting with berries.

"I know what yer thinkin', Adelaide Plume…but you get down here this minute!" Janie scolded. "We have enough mistletoe to fill the big barn's hayloft."

"Oh, we do not," Adelaide laughed as she scooted back toward the center of the tree.

"I still can't believe ya climbed that tree in yer stockin'ed feet," Janie laughed as Adelaide continued to find strong footholds and descend.

"Oh, these are my worst pair," Adelaide said. "They've already got a few holes in 'em and need darnin'. Besides, I couldn't climb this tree in my shoes. I really would break my neck then."

"Or at least yar ankle."

At the sound of Chance's voice, Adelaide paused in her descent—but only long enough to tame her temper. She had no doubt it had been Harvey who had managed to somehow make sure that Chance was standing under the oak tree just in time to see her jump down out of the tree in her holey stockings and most worn, faded green gingham day dress. Still, after the wonderful moments she'd spent in conversation with Chance one night the week before as they sat around the dying embers in the firepit, Adelaide knew she should not be humiliated. Chance understood Harvey was a mean-spirited skunk.

And so inhaling a deep breath to calm herself, Adelaide made the hop from the lowest oak tree branch to the ground. Turning around, she forced a smile of feigned indifference at standing before Chance in her stockinged feet, with a few tiny twigs in her hair and a pair of scissors tied around her waist.

"Good mornin', Chance," she greeted. "What're you doin' out at the big barn?"

"Oh, Mrs. Morgan sent her wee lad out to ask yar father if a couple of us hands could ride into town and help carry some tables and chairs into the barn," he explained, smiling at her. "Harvey and me finished that up…and yar brother thought you lassies might need some help out here, he did."

"And so he sent you to find out," Adelaide stated, blushing a little with mild embarrassment as well as frustration.

But Chance's smile broadened. He winked at her and said, "Oh, I volunteered, lass. Better to be out here with two bonny young ladies than settin' up chairs in the barn with yar brother and Mrs. Morgan's rambunctious lot of wee hellion sons, it is."

Adelaide and Janie both laughed, nodding with agreement.

"Oh, those Morgan boys are certainly somethin' to circumvent if a body is able," Janie offered.

"Unless a body is able to observe them from afar," Adelaide interjected. "Then they're more entertainin' than anything Mr. P.T. Barnum ever cooked up."

Chance chuckled, "I can just imagine it." He studied the large pile of mistletoe sprigs on the ground at Janie's feet. "Might I offer to carry yar plants for ya, lassies?" he asked. "That's a fine hill of mistletoe ya've harvested there." Glancing back to Adelaide, he inquired, "Are ye expectin' a lot of kissin' to be goin' on between folks this evenin' then?"

Adelaide glanced to Janie to see that her friend's cheeks were as rosy with blushing as her own.

"When…when my Grandma Plume—that'd be my pop's wife—moved near town," Adelaide began, "Grandma instituted the old practice of each couple pickin' a berry from the mistletoe sprig after they'd kissed beneath it. Once the berries are all gone, then the mistletoe loses its enchanted attributes, and the kissin' is supposed to stop. It's been the town tradition ever since, and, well, I...I..."

"Aye. Ya don't want to be runnin' out of berries before everyone has had his chance at kissin' tonight at the gatherin'," Chance finished. Stooping down and carefully gathering an armful of mistletoe bunches, he complimented, "That be very thoughtful of ya, lassy." He smiled at her, adding, "Yar a kind soul, ya are, Miss Adelaide. Now, where can I lay these down far ya, hmm?"

"I think it's sunny enough outside to keep us warm while we put the ribbons to them, don't you, Janie?" Adelaide asked.

"I think so," Janie concurred.

"So...if you'll just help us carry them to the picnic table nearest the big barn, we would be mighty grateful," she suggested.

"It'd be my pleasure," Chance agreed.

As Janie gathered up a few sprigs of mistletoe to carry to the table, Adelaide snatched up her shoes. Not even bothering to tighten the laces or tie them, she scrambled to gather some mistletoe herself, hurrying after Chance and Janie.

"Harvey tells me yar pop suggested this barn be built on the edge of the town far just such occasions as tonight's Christmas merriments," Chance remarked as he laid his armful of mistletoe on the weathered wooden picnic table.

"He did indeed," Adelaide affirmed with pride.

"Adelaide's Pop and Grandma Plume...well, there are those of us who believe that without them Oak Creek would never have become such a fruitful and friendly town," Janie said. "Why, my daddy says that if it weren't for Pop Plume, most of the farmers and cattle ranchers 'round these parts would've lost heart and moved on, instead of endurin' the hard times and droughts to a prosperous end." Janie pulled a roll of red ribbon from her apron pocket and, using the scissors tied around Adelaide's waist, cut a length of it.

"So, then…bein' that ye are his granddaughter," Chance addressed Adelaide, "you'd be the princess in these parts, ya would." Adelaide blushed as Chance continued, "I feel I'm a better sort of man, I do…far bein' in the presence of you, yar highness." He winked at her playfully, and Adelaide giggled with delight.

"Flattery is certainly one of yer gifts, Chance," she managed, blushing just a little.

Again Janie reached out, taking hold of the scissors tied at Adelaide's waist and using them to cut a length of red ribbon. "Oh, this will never do," she sighed. "I'm goin' in the barn to see if Mrs. Morgan has an extra pair on hand. It'll take us all day to tie up this mistletoe with only one pair." She handed the roll of red ribbon to Adelaide. "You keep goin', and I'll be right back."

"All right," Adelaide agreed.

She watched Janie turn and walk away, smoothing the back of her hair to make sure it was still pulled up nice and tidy. Janie wore a lovely blue calico dress and walked with more poise than any woman Adelaide had ever seen, and Adelaide exhaled a sigh of disappointment in herself as she looked down at her faded green gingham and unlaced shoes. She could only imagine what her hair looked like—for although she'd loosely braided it into one long braid that morning, she knew that the branches of the oak had tugged at it here and there and that there were small twigs and most likely remnants of dead leaves strewn through it.

Adelaide looked up to find Chance grinning at her—an amused, knowing grin—as if he knew exactly what she was thinking. Oh, but he was the handsomest man on earth! She knew he was! And it was humiliating to be standing before him looking so tattered and childish.

And yet she thought of the new red dress she'd finished for herself the day before—the fact that Janie was going to help her pull her hair up—and she felt a smile spread across her face. *Just you wait, Chance Flannery! Just you wait until you see me tonight!*

"You're grinnin' like a possum eatin' a sweet potato," Adelaide offered with amusement. "What kind of mischief is in your mind?" The fact was, his impish grin had caused Adelaide's heart to start beating as fast as hummingbird wings, and she must know if she was the cause of the sparkle in his beautiful blue eyes or not. Did Chance appear tickled because she looked such a ragamuffin sight? Or was there something else? She hoped with all her heart there was something else.

"'Twas I was hopin' yar friend would leave, I was," he admitted.

"Y-you were?" Adelaide asked in a whisper, her heart beating even faster.

"Aye, lass," Chance answered, lowering his voice, "far at last, a scheme has struck me mind where yar skunk of a brother is concerned, it has."

Adelaide's eyes widened, her heart feeling as if it had stopped for a moment. She didn't know whether to be overjoyed that Chance did not seemed amused by her tatterdemalioned, raggedy scarecrow appearance or sad that he had not confessed a secreted love for her.

Yet feigning a serenity she did not feel, Adelaide prodded, "Well, do tell! I'm as curious as a dog hearin' sounds from a crate."

Chance's dazzling smile broadened. "Ye know the Widow Doyle, don't ya, lass?" he began.

"Oh, of course!" Adelaide exclaimed at the mention of the kindest lady in town. "She's as sweet as cream and sugar…and probably a hundred years old, at least."

Chance nodded. "Aye," he affirmed. "Well, I'm quite taken with her, I am. She's been so kind to me since I come to town—like a grandmother, she is—and I hold her with deep affection. I try to check in on her a couple of times a week, I do."

Again Adelaide's heart leapt into her bosom—this time with loving approval. Mrs. Doyle was alone in the world; even her six children had passed through the veil and into heaven before her. During months of warm weather, Adelaide would often ride Roger over to visit with Mrs. Doyle, who loved the pampered steer as if he were her own. Adelaide adored Mrs. Doyle, and knowing that Chance knew her, and obviously visited her on occasion—well, she instantly fell even more in love with the handsome man.

"And I think our dear Mrs. Doyle would help us with some tomfoolery I've just envisioned far yar brother, Harvey," Chance offered.

"Ooo! What tomfoolery would that be?" Adelaide giggled, excited by the prospect of giving Harvey what he deserved for once.

Chuckling, Chance picked up a small bunch of mistletoe from the table, holding it up and nodding as he inquired, "Yar hangin' up these kissin' plant bits in every doorway of the barn, are ye?"

"Yes," Adelaide affirmed as her excitement rose. "And in other places in the barn, as well."

"And yar brother, Harvey, though he be a skunk…he's a good enough man that he would never refuse a kiss, no matter what woman might catch him beneath it, he wouldn't," Chance stated.

Adelaide bit her lip with anticipation—for she knew what Chance would say next.

"Thus, we pull Mrs. Doyle into our plot...and be sure and certain that one of us lures Harvey to standin' beneath a sprig of this red-ribboned greenery..."

Goose bumps raced over Adelaide's arms at the sound of Chance's trilling Rs in describing the mistletoe.

"And when the trap is set, Mrs. Doyle joins yar brother beneath it, and bein' that there must be somethin' of a gentleman in him..."

Chance began to laugh in his throat, and Adelaide finished, "He would never refuse her...and will have to kiss her!"

Waves of gleeful chortling overtook her at once, and in mere moments more, she and Chance were each laughing with such merriment at anticipating Harvey's being forced to kiss dear, sweet, but very elderly Mrs. Doyle, neither of them could speak.

Their shared laughter only diminished when Fordy rode up, reining in next to them.

"What's got you two cacklin' like a coupla hens?" he inquired, a light laughter escaping his throat as the contagiousness of their hilarity infected him.

"Oh, nothin' worth the mentionin'," Chance managed. He inhaled a deep breath, exhaling it with the remnants of one last chuckle. "Are ye here to help with the settin' up, Fordy?"

Fordy glanced to Adelaide, and she did not miss the worry in his eyes.

"No," Fordy answered. "Um...Pop wants everyone back to the ranch," he stammered. "There's a...a coupla heifers gone missin' from Mr. Worden's place, and...uh...Pa wants us to help find 'em."

"I'm right behind ya then," Chance said, his smile vanishing like pond ice in summer.

"Good," Fordy said with a nod. He looked to Adelaide then, forced a happy smile, and remarked, "I see you and Janie have enough mistletoe there to marry off ever'body in town."

"Oh, it's not so much, Fordy," Adelaide dismissed. "But you be sure you catch yerself a pretty girl underneath it tonight, all right?"

Fordy chuckled. "All right, little sister, I will." Turning his horse, he called, "See you at home, Chance." Then he clicked his tongue and set off at a steady canter.

"Mr. Worden has lost more cattle, Chance," Adelaide whispered as fear began to nest in her mind. "Rustlers are dangerous and…"

It was the pleasing sensation of Chance's strong hands on her shoulders that kept Adelaide's fear from rising to panic.

"Now don't ya be worryin' about that, lassy," Chance soothed, his voice low and comforting like warm milk and cinnamon pudding on a cold night. "They'll move on, they will. Or we'll round them up and jail them." He smiled at her, winked, and said, "You just take yar red ribbon there, get that kissin' shrub up in the big barn, and think about yar skunk of a brother kissin' Mrs. Doyle beneath it."

"I'll try," Adelaide promised.

Chance's smile broadened. "If our plot is successful, not only will Harvey be gettin' back a little that he gave…but I'm thinkin' Mrs. Doyle will have a Christmas kiss the like she's not had in decades, she will."

Adelaide's heart indeed lightened at the thought of Mrs. Doyle receiving a Christmas kiss from a handsome cowboy, and she nodded with happy anticipation.

"Found some!" Janie hollered as she approached from the barn, triumphantly waving a set of scissors over her head.

Lowering his voice, Chance suggested, "And…bein' that yar friend is a bit smitten by yar skunky brother…"

"I would never tell anyone about our scheme, Chance," Adelaide assured him, still relishing his touch at her shoulders, "least of all Janie."

"Well, then, lassy," he breathed, dropping his hands from her shoulders. She noted she felt colder once he'd released her. "I'll get to searchin' for Mr. Worden's heifers, I will…smilin' all the day long with eager expectancy that tonight's Christmas festivities will be like none other. You have fun decoratin' that big barn, lassy."

"I will," Adelaide confirmed.

She watched as he turned and hurriedly strode to where his horse was hitched near the big barn.

"My, my, my," Janie teased, smiling. "I am so glad I thought to fetch another pair of scissors. Looks like you and Mr. Chance Flannery were sharin' cheerful conversation."

"Yes, we were!" Adelaide giggled. The delight inside her over Chance's attention, and scheme to give Harvey a mistletoe kiss he'd never forget, was euphoric—even for the lingering worry over the ghostlike rustlers prowling nearby.

Janie giggled as well, offering, "Well, maybe you'll find yerself standin' under one of these with Chance tonight." She held up a small mistletoe bunch, waving it toward Adelaide before she picked up one length of ribbon and began tying it through the kissing plant.

Even though her heart felt as if it were going to fly up and out the top of her head at the thought of receiving a kiss from Chance, Adelaide attempted to appear unaffected by Janie's teasing.

"Oh, maybe," she sighed. "Though the more probable outcome would be me findin' myself under the mistletoe with some other cowboy…like Boney Bob or Cliff."

"Don't even say such things out loud, Addy!" Janie said, wrinkling her nose in a grimace. "Poor Cliff is uglier than a mud fence, and Boney Bob…well, there ain't nothin' at all to him but skin and bones! I mean, they're both such nice men, but, well…a woman needs to be attracted to the man she kisses, doesn't she? I mean…oh, I'm just a terrible person! How could I say such cruel things?"

Adelaide laughed quietly, amused by the way Janie always took to immediate repenting whenever she'd said something that wasn't kind.

"I know what ya meant, Janie," Adelaide soothed. "There's someone for everyone, and a body does need to find her someone attractive. I'm certain there are plenty of girls in the world that would find Boney Bob and Cliff to be just as handsome and dashin' as you find Harvey and I find Chance to be."

"*Truly?*" Janie squeaked, obviously skeptical.

"Yes!" Adelaide laughed. "Now quit worryin' on the fact you don't think Boney and Cliff are handsome and help me get this mistletoe tied up, or no one will be enjoying Christmas kisses tonight."

"All right," Janie giggled.

As Adelaide and Janie worked cutting ribbon and adorning bunches of mistletoe with it, Janie suddenly declared, "Oh, you see the things Mrs. Morgan is puttin' out for the bazaar tonight? It's certain to be our best bazaar ever…or at least in my memory."

"I'm glad," Addy said. "Although I hope my pillowcases don't suffer by comparison to all the other things folks have made."

"Oh, not at all! They turned out beautifully, Addy—just beautifully!" Janie sighed with contentment, adding, "I just love Christmastime. And isn't there to be a full moon soon?"

Adelaide nodded. "Christmas Eve," she confirmed.

"A full moon on Christmas Eve," Janie sighed once more. "I can't imagine any moon bein' more wonderful than a full moon on Christmas Eve."

"Me neither," Adelaide fibbed. A week before, she would've wholeheartedly agreed that no moon could ever be more marvelous than a full moon on Christmas Eve. But that was before she'd spent a blissful little while lazing under a nearly full moon with an ember-laden fire before her and delectable Chance Flannery at her side.

CHAPER FIVE

Oak Creek's big barn glowed like a beacon, guiding townsfolk to a haven of warmth and merriment. Although the *Farmers' Almanac* promised heavy snow on Christmas Day, the night of the Christmas bazaar and dance was crisp and clear. A nearly full, silvery moon watched over infinite twinkling stars, and Adelaide thought there could never be a more perfect night for a happy gathering of families and friends.

The diverse aromas—of freshly baked pumpkin and apple pies, breads, cookies, and cakes mingled with the savory scents of hearty beef stews, sugar-glazed hams, roasted chickens, potatoes, onions, and spiced apple cider—wafted from the brightly lit barn and into the cool air without. Adelaide mused that if the warm light of the barn hadn't managed to tempt every man, woman, and child inside, the heavenly bouquet of the delicious edibles on the air undoubtedly would.

As Dean halted the horse and buggy he and Adelaide had taken to the big barn, he smiled, noting, "The big barn sure looks invitin', Addy."

"It sure does," Adelaide agreed. Excitement had been mounting in her since the moment she and her daddy had left home in the buggy. Pop, her brothers, Chance, and the other cowboys had left on horseback a few minutes earlier. Therefore, only Janie and her daddy had seen her new red dress and her hair pulled up into a perfect coiffure. She felt her hands begin to tremble as her daddy hopped down from the buggy and secured the lines to the hitching post.

"Good girl," Dean soothed, patting the bay horse, Trudy, between the ears. "We'll try to get ya home before it gets too awful cold there, Trudy."

Ever the gentleman, Adelaide's father strode to her side of the buggy, offering her his hand to assist her in disembarking.

"Thank you, Daddy," she said as she stepped off the buggy step and onto the ground.

"Yer welcome, sweetheart," Dean said, smiling at her.

Adelaide noticed the rather wistful look in his handsome eyes— as if he were battling joy and sadness at the same time.

"Yer so beautiful, Adelaide," he complimented. "Ya always are, of course. But ya look so grown up tonight." She noted the moisture in her father's eyes, and it pricked her heart with uncomfortable empathy for his mingled emotions.

"Thank you, Daddy," she managed, however. "And yer gonna set all the ladies to swoonin' tonight in yer new vest and tie!" She reached out, straightening the knot of her daddy's tie, and wondered why he'd never remarried. Her mother had been gone for so very long, and all the ladies in town thought Dean Plume was the handsomest man in the county. Someday Adelaide and her two brothers would marry and leave home, and Adelaide winced, feeling pain again as she thought of her father and Pop sitting alone at the supper table every night.

"Now don't you go slatherin' me with flattery, little girl. I ain't comfortable with it," he chuckled. Then, taking her arm and linking it with his, he added, "But don't *you* go breakin' too many hearts tonight, darlin'. Why, that red dress is gonna draw cowboys to you like flies to honey!"

"Oh Daddy, don't be silly," Adelaide giggled. After all, she was only hoping the red dress and her fancied-up hair would draw in one cowboy—Chance Flannery. "And by the way, Daddy…ya know I coulda ridden in tonight."

"On Roger? It'd take ya 'til tomorrow to get here," Dean chuckled.

Adelaide laughed, "Not on Roger! I'd have ridden Georgie, of course."

"And arrived lookin' like somethin' the cat dragged in," Dean reminded with a smile. "Nope! My daughter is a princess and deserves to be buggied to the ball. And I wouldn't have it any other way." He leaned over, placing an affectionate kiss to Adelaide's temple.

"Thank you, Daddy," Adelaide offered with sincere gratitude. For truth be told, she'd been too bashful to ask her daddy if she could take the buggy into town that night—even though she'd known riding in on Georgie might have been detrimental to her hairdressing. In the end, however, she hadn't had to ask. Dean Plume was a gentleman where any woman was concerned, especially his daughter, and he'd hitched up the buggy without even telling Adelaide until it was almost time to leave.

"Yer welcome, sweet pea," Dean said as they walked.

Stepping into the barn was almost like entering heaven. The full inside of the big barn was slathered in Christmas beauty! Pine boughs and wreaths embellished with red ribbons and sugar cookies were strewn on every inner wall. Flickering lamps and candles festooned with holly topped every table and low ceiling beam, providing the much-needed light for the evening's revelry. Garlands of strung popcorn and red cranberries (a rare treat indeed in Oak Creek and sent all the way from Mrs. Morgan's sister in Massachusetts) clung to the two large Christmas trees that had been brought in, set at opposing ends of the barn and decorated with fruit, nuts, and gingerbread. Long tables laden with items crafted by townsfolk and donated to the Christmas bazaar stood to one side of the room—tables that, when emptied of items, would be piled high with the foodstuffs that sat behind them, waiting to tempt everyone's palate. And of course each door threshold and window frame was festooned with a thick bundle of mistletoe hanging overhead. Even here and there along the low ceiling beams hung bouquets of mistletoe thick with white berries. To Adelaide, it was the most stunning vision of Christmas cheerfulness imaginable.

Dean took Adelaide's coat from around her shoulders, hanging it on an empty hook near the door through which they'd entered.

"Thank you, Daddy," she said. "Oh, isn't it *so* beautiful?"

"It's lovely," he answered, smiling down at her.

In fact, Adelaide was so overwhelmed with delight at seeing the big barn so awash in Christmas beauty, she did not even notice that everyone had turned and was staring at her and her father.

Her father enthusiastically called, "Merry Christmas!" and was met with a barrage of Merry Christmases in return, and then Adelaide's attention was finally diverted from awe in the glorious decoration to smiling at Janie as her friend hurried toward her.

"Oh, you look perfect, Addy!" Janie greeted, taking Adelaide's hands in her own. "Just perfect."

"Do I?" Adelaide inquired, still feeling quite uncertain of herself. After all, she'd never worn her hair up—never worn a dress with a

V-line bodice that only just barely capped her shoulders, leaving her entire clavicle unveiled.

"Oh, without question!" Janie assured in a whisper.

"Have a good time, ladies," Dean chuckled as he strode away, leaving the two young ladies to their whispers and giggles.

"Thank you, Mr. Plume," Janie said. "This red is just so…well, Addy, it just looks lovely. Just lovely!" Janie gushed as she studied Adelaide's dress.

"Not as lovely as this pink yer wearin'!" Adelaide exclaimed as she studied Janie's beautiful pink dress, her upswept golden hair, and her warm brown eyes.

"Well, we both look our best," Janie giggled. "Our *grown-up* best," she added in a whisper. "And you'll never believe what else."

"What?" Adelaide inquired, curious—even as she looked beyond Janie, scanning the room for a glimpse of Chance.

"Harvey already kissed me under the mistletoe!" Janie breathed.

"He did?" Adelaide asked, delighted to see her friend so euphoric.

"Yes! He did! And oh, Addy, it was…well, I suppose it was wonderful," Janie offered. "I've never been kissed like that before…sort of sloppy and wet—you know, the way we caught Ike Wilson and Mary Eaten kissin' out back of the general store last summer. And it wasn't a terribly long kiss…so I think it was wonderful, but I was such a Nervous Nelly, I can't remember!"

Janie giggled, and Addy—although rather irked at thinking of her brother kissing Janie the way Ike Wilson had been kissing Mary Eaten the summer before—smiled and nodded in sharing her friend's delight.

"I'll tell you all about it later," Janie said then. "But for now, we best head over to the tables and see if there's anything we'd like to buy. It looks like things are gettin' sold pretty quick."

"All right," Adelaide agreed. "But...have ya seen Chance yet?"

"Oh my, yes!" Janie whispered as they moved toward the tables of bazaar items. "And he looks good enough to eat—all fancied up in his fresh white shirt, black vest, and green tie. You'll have a hard time not faintin' away in a swoon when ya see him."

Adelaide blushed at the mere thought of how handsome Chance would look dressed up and standing in the firelight.

"Let me see. Last time I saw him, he was just over there..." Janie mumbled as she looked to the other end of the big barn. "There he is!" she whispered. "Over there by the Christmas tree at the far end. Do ya see him?"

Looking in the direction Janie was, Adelaide drew in a quiet gasp of admiration as her gaze fell to Chance. He was standing near the far Christmas tree steeped in conversation with Mrs. Doyle—and oh, did he look handsome! He wore a dark blue pair of copper-riveted pants, fresh white shirt, black vest, and dark green tie—just as Janie had described. However, Adelaide had not expected that seeing Chance shined up a like a new penny would cause her knees to weaken and nearly take her breath away. In fact, the sight of Chance looking so alluring amid all the Christmas trimmings literally made her mouth water.

"Oh goodness!" she whispered, breathless. "Janie, I think my heart is gonna leap right out of my bosom."

Janie giggled. "I figured it might," she admitted. "But before it does, let's go see what lovely things there are to buy...and if yer pillowcases and my tatted towels have sold yet. All right?"

"Y-yes...let's," Adelaide stammered, still awed by how attractive Chance was. Not that he wasn't always mouth-wateringly handsome, but something about him standing near a Christmas tree, dressed in his finest, and kindly conversing with Mrs. Doyle—who was often somewhat neglected socially because of her age and widowhood—made him even more fascinating somehow.

Nevertheless, as she and Janie hurried to the tables to peruse the items there, Adelaide's heart began to hammer with anxiety. After all, no matter how pretty her red dress was and no matter how much more mature she looked with her hair up—well, Chance was still a full-grown man who could no doubt win the heart and affections of any woman in town. And judging from the way the other eligible, unmarried young ladies in town were all staring toward the far end of the barn where Chance stood, Adelaide wasn't alone in her admiration of him.

"What if he thinks I look ridiculous, Janie?" she asked her friend in a hushed voice.

"Oh, don't be silly," Janie assured her as she studied a lovely doily. "Once he sees you lookin' yer age, you'll be lucky if he doesn't whisk ya out of the barn to have his way with you."

"Shhh!" Adelaide scolded, blushing. "I cannot believe you would say such a thing, Jane Higginson! What would yer mother think?"

But Janie shrugged. "What would my mother think if she knew I'd been kissed the way Harvey kissed me tonight? Why, she'd turn us Catholic and send me off to be a nun in a heartbeat, that's what."

Adelaide smiled, adoring her friend all the more for her occasional scandalous remarks.

"And look at the way all the other girls here are gawkin' at Chance," Adelaide grumbled. "After this, every female from here to Mexico is gonna try winnin' him."

"It won't matter," Janie answered, "'cause once he sets eyes on you in that red dress, he'll never notice another woman for as long as he lives."

"Now you know that's not true," Adelaide argued, her heart feeling heavy. She hadn't even thought of the competition she might encounter when trying to procure Chance's attention.

"It *is* true, so stop yer worryin'," Janie demanded.

Adelaide would not stop worrying, but she would stop worrying aloud to Janie. For one thing, she wanted her friend to enjoy the evening, even if Adelaide was nervous. And for another, she surmised that Janie couldn't wholly understand Adelaide's anxiety. After all, Janie had already received her dream kiss under the mistletoe—from Harvey. Therefore, even though the thought of Harvey the Skunk slobbering all over Janie made Adelaide's stomach turn, she would never think of spoiling her dearest friend's bliss.

"This doily is just so pretty," Janie remarked as she continued to scrutinize it. "I would bet my hind end that ol' Mrs. Doyle made it, wouldn't you?"

"Oh, I'm sure she did," Adelaide agreed without even looking at the doily—for something else had wholly captured her attention.

The most beautiful little doll cradle Adelaide had ever seen was sitting on the table near the doily. Simple in its design, yet showing skilled craftsmanship, the little cradle's sides, headboard, and footboard had been perfectly sanded to be smooth as mink and stained a pretty dark walnut. Instantly Adelaide began imagining the tiny bedding she could make to fit it—a soft downy mattress, pillow, sheet, and tiny quilt made from some of the cloth scraps her mother had saved before Adelaide had been born. Her heart warmed in her bosom in thinking of her greatest treasure—her mother's childhood doll—finally having a proper place to lay her tiny head each night.

When Adelaide turned eight years old, her father had entrusted her with a true treasure: her mother's childhood doll. Adelaide's mother's doll, with porcelain head, arms, and legs and cloth body, had been a Christmas gift to her mother on her own eighth birthday. Adelaide's father explained that her mother had always planned to give the doll—lovingly named Fanny by her mother—to her own daughter one day. And from that moment forward, her mother's doll had been Adelaide's most cherished possession.

Still, and forever, dressed in the lovely pink gown her mother had lovingly hand-stitched for the doll just before she'd married Adelaide's father, Fanny had been tucked away in the wooden chest at the foot of Adelaide's bed for years. Comfortable sleeping on the scraps of fabric her mother had been saving to make quilts and clothes for her children, Fanny was well protected. And yet often Adelaide would feel unsettled with the fact that the doll was in the chest—worrying that Fanny couldn't breathe in such a closed space.

But now, right there before her on one of the bazaar tables, sat the loveliest doll cradle, with proportions perfect for a doll Fanny's size. Silly as it sounded even in her own mind, Adelaide felt as if the cradle were meant to be hers. So without even checking the price assigned to it, Adelaide snatched up the cradle and the little piece of cost-paper next to it and hurried to where Mrs. Morgan stood collecting payments.

"Oh, isn't this just darlin'?" Mrs. Morgan exclaimed, looking at the cradle as Adelaide handed her the small slip of paper with the bazaar price written on it. "The moment I saw it, I just *knew* someone would snatch it up for a special dolly." Mrs. Morgan winked at Adelaide, adding, "Is this a gift for a little girl in town?"

"No…it's for me. Well, for my mama's doll," Adelaide explained. "She's been in a chest at the foot of my bed for years now, and I saw this…and just knew it was meant for her."

Mrs. Morgan's smile broadened, although Adelaide did not miss the expression of sympathy in her eyes. "Oh, that's…that's so sweet, Adelaide," she offered. "That just tugs at my heartstrings." Mrs. Morgan looked at the price written on the paper. "Well, I hope it's not too rich a price for ya, honey. I priced it at a dollar. After all, it is such a nice little cradle."

"And I'm more than happy to pay that much, Mrs. Morgan," Adelaide assured the woman. "It is so perfect!"

Setting the cradle down for a moment and reaching into the small purse hanging at her wrist, Adelaide retrieved a dollar coin, handing it to Mrs. Morgan.

Accepting the coin, Mrs. Morgan replied, "Thank you! And the future Oak Creek library is grateful for yer contribution, Adelaide Plume." Placing the coin in a small lockbox behind her, the woman suggested, "Why don't I get your pa to haul that home for ya?"

"Oh, that's all right, Mrs. Morgan," Adelaide countered. She snatched up the cradle, fearing that somehow someone else would abscond with it. "I'll just run it on out to the buggy this minute."

Adelaide turned to leave and found herself face to face with Chance! She blushed crimson as he smiled at her and then glanced down to the cradle in her arms. After all her efforts in primping and preening—after wearing a red gown that somewhat exhibited her entire neck and clavicle, after so much hard work in order to catch Chance's eye and hope he would finally see her as a woman instead of a girl—there she stood, clutching a doll's cradle!

"Ya should've told me ya wanted the cradle, lassy," he said, still smiling at her. "I'd have given it to ye for free, I would've."

Adelaide's eyes widened. "Y-you made this, Chance?" she stammered, utterly stunned.

"Aye, lass," he answered with a nod. "It's not a fancy one, far it's all I could manage with the tools available in yar father's barn. But it's a sweet little thing, it is. I hope ye find a use far it."

"Oh...oh, I already have," Adelaide admitted. "And I'm happy to pay for it. It's beautiful and perfect! And I am glad I could contribute to our hopes of one day havin' a library."

"Ah, yar a kind young lady, ya are, Miss Adelaide," Chance complimented. "Would ya like me to carry it home for ya?"

"I...uh...I was just gonna run it on out to the buggy," she answered. "Daddy and I came in the buggy."

She was flustered! He was so very handsome—as he always was.

"Let me take it out far ya please," he said. Then lowering his voice, he leaned closer to her, whispering, "Far I wouldn't want ye to miss Mrs. Doyle's mischief."

Adelaide gasped with glee. "She's gonna do it soon?" she inquired with a giggle.

"As soon as the food is brung, she plans," Chance assured. "And I wouldn't want ye to miss it, lass. So let me run that cradle out for ye, so that ye can keep an eye out in case the mischief is sooner than later. I wouldn't want ye to miss it. Not far anything."

"Thank you," Adelaide sighed, handing the cradle to Chance. "You know our buggy, don't ya?"

Chance winked at her, saying, "Aye, lass. As well as I know who the prettiest girl in this Christmas barn is, I do."

"Wh-who? M-me?" Adelaide stammered, uncertain as to whether his wink was meant for her—because she was the prettiest girl in the barn or simply because there was a prettier girl in the barn and he knew her.

Chance laughed, his blue eyes bright with merriment. "Of course, lassy!" He shook his head as his amusement lingered. "Aye, but yar a humble thing."

As Adelaide tried to remain calm—tried not to swoon away in the bliss of his compliment and notice—Chance lowered his voice again and charged, "I'll run this outside, while you keep a watch over Mrs. Doyle, aye?"

"Oh my, yes!" Adelaide giggled.

Chance winked at her once more, adding, "With any luck, that brother of yars will get his, and this will be the merriest Christmas ya've ever had."

"Yes!" Adelaide agreed with an excited nod.

Chance was off to the buggy then—and very quickly. Adelaide knew he did not want to miss the mischief he had put Mrs. Doyle up to either.

Adelaide watched the side barn door through which Chance had disappeared with the cradle. She was anxious—worried that Mrs. Doyle might step up the timing of their scheme. Still, he wasn't gone more than a minute or two, and Adelaide sighed with relief when she saw him step back into the barn and nod at her in confirming her cradle was safe.

Her relief changed to frustration, however, when, one moment after Chance had reentered the barn, he was met with a bombardment of girls from Oak Creek. Young ladies older than Adelaide, young ladies near her age, and even a few younger than she were gathered round Chance Flannery as if they had been starving for weeks and he were cake!

"I'll have this doily, Mrs. Morgan," Janie said to Mrs. Morgan where they stood behind Adelaide.

"Oh, this is a lovely one, Janie. Just lovely!" Mrs. Morgan cooed. "It'll look nice in yer parlor once yer married and settled in one day."

"I hope so," Jamie responded kindly. "Thank you, Mrs. Morgan." Moving to stand next to Adelaide, Janie leaned toward her and whispered, "Looks like yer secret is no longer a secret. You'd think they'd never seen a good-lookin' man before!"

"They haven't seen one," Adelaide pointed out. "Not one as good-lookin' as Chance, anyway."

As if reading Adelaide's mind, Janie put a comforting arm around her friend. "Don't you worry a minute over it, Addy," she encouraged. "There's not a girl in town as pretty as you, as smart as you, or as interestin'. I saw Chance talkin' with ya just now…and I swear he was close to droolin' over you!"

"Oh, he was not," Adelaide playfully argued, remembering Chance's telling her that he knew she was the prettiest girl in the Christmas barn.

"He was so!" Janie countered. "Why, I just know he's gonna capture ya under one of our mistletoe traps tonight, Addy. I just know it!"

Just then, Mrs. Morgan hollered, "Would some of you menfolk help with movin' these tables around so we can start settin' up the victuals please?"

Adelaide smiled, feeling better as Chance politely nodded to each young woman hovering around him and headed toward where Mrs. Morgan stood, barking orders.

Maybe Janie was right. Maybe heaven would smile down on Adelaide Plume and Chance *would* catch her under the mistletoe and kiss her. After all, if the man could talk Mrs. Doyle into plotting against Harvey with him, anything was possible!

CHAPTER SIX

Adelaide couldn't help but smile as she watched Chance assist in rearranging tables, so that the food could be brought in and so that folks would have places to sit in order to enjoy it. Of course, Adelaide adored observing anything Chance was doing. Nevertheless, studying him in such a festive atmosphere—well, even his mildest movements set her heart to fluttering.

An audible sigh of disenchantment from Janie distracted Adelaide, however, and she glanced to her friend standing beside her to see Janie's brows knit together in a slight frown.

"What's the matter, Janie?" Adelaide inquired. It stood to reason that Janie should be as happy watching Harvey as Adelaide watching Chance, since Harvey, Fordy, Adelaide's father, and Pop were helping with the tables as well. Yet it was obvious she was not.

Janie shrugged, exhaling another sigh. "I don't know, Addy," she answered. "I just feel…well, rather restless and…downright dissatisfied for some reason."

"Dissatisfied about what?" Adelaide pressed. She didn't want Janie to be anything less than gleeful. After all, the barn was beautiful and warm in its Christmas regalia—and hadn't Janie known a dream come true in having been kissed beneath the mistletoe by Harvey? Even if he were a skunk?

Again Janie shrugged. "I-I really don't know. I can't put my finger on it at all. I mean, shouldn't I just be jumpin' over the moon with delight 'cause Harvey kissed me?"

"One would think, yes," Adelaide ventured.

"Well, I'm not," Janie admitted in a whisper. "Whenever I think about it...well, my stomach kind of knots up for some reason."

Adelaide exhaled her own sigh then. Only her sigh was that of relief.

"Sounds to me that, after all these years of bein' puppy-eyed and sweet over Harvey, you've discovered ya don't love him, or even like him, as much as ya thought ya did," Adelaide kindly offered. " 'Cause it seems to me that if you *did*, you certainly would feel like jumpin' over the moon...instead of havin' knots in yer stomach."

Janie looked to Adelaide, her frown deepening. "That's what I'm afraid of," she admitted. "But still," she added, straightening her posture, "maybe it's just the jitters. Maybe it's just because it was our first kiss and all and I was just too awful nervous to...to enjoy it."

"Maybe ya oughta kiss him again," Adelaide suggested, hoping that a second kiss would tie Janie's stomach in worse knots and she'd finally realize what a slobbering skunk Harvey really was. "You won't be as anxious the second time...and then maybe you can tell for certain whether or not you truly like Harvey the way you think you do...or did."

Janie's eyes widened with astonishment. "Well, how on earth do you expect me to kiss him again, Adelaide Plume? It's not like he's gonna catch me under the mistletoe more'n once this evenin'."

"Why ever not?" Adelaide giggled, taking Janie's arm. "Believe me, I'm sure with a little schemin', we can make it happen! And without anyone bein' the wiser too."

"Oh? And how do you suggest we make it happen?" Janie asked in a whisper.

"Oh, don't you worry, Miss Jane Higginson," Adelaide assured her. "It just so happens that I have a little experience in these matters already."

"What are you goin' on about, Addy?" Janie asked, obviously intrigued.

"Well, ya know how I told you that Chance suggested I give Harvey back a little of what he gives me, hmmm?" Adelaide confided.

"Yes…" Janie affirmed.

"Well, look yonder," she said, nodding toward the place where Harvey stood, arms folded across his chest, nodding as he silently counted the chairs he'd just finished setting up along one side of a table.

"At Harvey?" Janie whispered.

"Yep," Adelaide answered. "Now look what's hanging from the low ceiling beam just above him."

Janie glanced up and, seeing the large bunch of red-ribboned mistletoe, smiled, asking, "Are you suggestin' that I—"

"No!" Adelaide quietly exclaimed. "At least not yet."

"Then what on earth—"

"Just wait a moment…just one more moment," Adelaide prodded as she watched the Widow Doyle approaching Harvey from behind—her cane click-click-clicking on the floor as she went.

Adelaide looked to Chance, who was standing a short distance away, watching Mrs. Doyle as well. Chance looked to her, smiled, and winked, and Adelaide knew the moment was upon them.

Adelaide and Janie watched in mesmerized silence as the kind, gray-haired old lady walked up behind Harvey, reached out, and tapped him on the shoulder.

Out of the corner of her eye, Adelaide saw Janie quietly gasp and clamp a hand over her mouth.

"Mr. Plume?" Mrs. Doyle inquired when Harvey turned around to see who had tapped his shoulder.

"Well, hello there, Mrs. Doyle," Harvey greeted with a smile. "Merry Christmas! And what can I do for you this fine evenin'?"

Without speaking, Mrs. Doyle raised one crooked, gnarled, old index finger and pointed up.

"What's that, Mrs. Doyle?" Harvey asked.

Again Mrs. Doyle pointed up, this time speaking. "We're under the mistletoe, honey lamb. And you know the rules, don't ya?"

Adelaide bit her lower lip to keep from bursting into giggles. Oh, Mrs. Doyle was by no means a homely woman, but she was elderly, and Adelaide knew Harvey had no desire to kiss her—especially on the lips.

"Oh, um…oh, ha ha!" Harvey nervously stammered. "I…uh…I sure do know the rules."

"Well, I'm waitin' for my Christmas kiss then, young Mr. Plume," Mrs. Doyle reminded.

"Oh, uh…of…of course, Mrs. Doyle," Harvey choked. "I'd be honored."

But as Harvey bent down, obviously intending to kiss Mrs. Doyle on one cheek, Mrs. Doyle quickly dropped her cane, reached out, and took hold of Harvey's tie (with a much stronger grip than Adelaide thought she was capable). Yanking hard on Harvey's tie until he was forced to bend down, Mrs. Doyle then put her free hand and arm around his neck and kissed him! But it was no tender, sweet, under-the-mistletoe kiss like most Adelaide had seen. No indeed!

As Mrs. Doyle ground her mouth to Harvey's, kissing him with full as much passion as Ike Wilson had kissed Mary Eaten behind the general store last summer, Janie breathed, "Good golly, my garters!" as Adelaide struggled to restrain her laughter.

After long moments of Mrs. Doyle's affections, Harvey reached, gently pushing at the old woman's shoulders.

As he attempted to pull away, the plucky widow took hold of his tie once more, chirping, "I ain't done with you yet, handsome," and took to kissing him just as thoroughly as she had the first time.

Adelaide looked to Chance to see him stooped over with his fists on his knees, trying not to laugh out loud. He glanced up to Adelaide, nodding with approval and wiping a tear of mirth from the corner of each of his beautiful and very merry eyes.

A quiet hush had fallen over the inside of the barn, and Adelaide looked around to see that the attention of every soul was fixated on Harvey and Mrs. Doyle and their impassioned, albeit one-sided, kissing.

And when the old filly at last released Harvey, such a roar of applause and hooting and hollering of approval went up that Adelaide thought the big barn had never held such a burst of merriment!

At last Mrs. Doyle turned to the largest group of onlookers, cheerfully calling, "Merry Christmas, everyone!"

Dean Plume, still laughing, hurried to her side, retrieved her cane, and put a strong arm around her shoulders to steady her.

"Merry Christmas!" came the shouts of cheerful hearts in return.

For his part, Harvey looked like a cat that had only just missed being run over by a stagecoach. His face was as red as a summer beet, and as he straightened his tie, he nodded this way and that, attempting to appear composed—unruffled by Mrs. Doyle's affections.

"All right, everyone," Mrs. Morgan hollered. "Let's eat!"

Chance winked at Adelaide as he hurried toward Mrs. Doyle. "Aye, Mrs. Doyle," Adelaide heard him say, "might I find ye a seat and gather a plate of food far ya this evenin'?"

"Of course, you can, sweetheart," Mrs. Doyle agreed, patting his cheek with affection. "I find I'm plumb tuckered out for some reason or another."

"Yes, ma'am," Chance chuckled.

"Are you tellin' me that you planned all that?" Janie whispered.

Adelaide looked to her friend, anxious that Janie might be upset with her for being involved in the shenanigans meant to embarrass Harvey.

"Yes...me and Chance," Adelaide whispered. "Are ya angry, Janie? Please don't be angry! You know Harvey deserves what he gets."

But Janie's eyes were bright with mirth, and she shook her head. "How could I be mad? I've never seen anything so...well, so shocking and yet funny at the same time!"

Adelaide exhaled a sigh of relief. "Oh good. I was so afraid you'd be mad." Then, thinking of how vicious any reprisal from Harvey would be if he were to find out Chance conceived the scheme and Adelaide supported it, she added, "But you can never tell anyone, Janie! Especially not Harvey! Please!"

Taking Adelaide's hand in her own, Janie promised, "I would never tell Harvey! I will never tell a livin' soul unless you gave permission for me to." She giggled again, adding, "And now I see why ya think you can get Harvey to meet me under the mistletoe for a second kiss tonight. And I'll never doubt ya on anything ever again, Adelaide Plume! Not ever!"

"I don't know, Angus," Pop said, addressing Mr. Worden. "But after Christmas, we gotta do somethin' about it."

"It can't be a big operation," Dean offered, "else they'd be takin' more'n two or three head each time."

Adelaide listened intently to the conversation her father, grandfather, and brothers were having with Mr. Worden. Both Mr. Worden's cowboys and the Plumes had been unable to catch even a glimpse of the rustlers suspected of stealing cattle. And although the discussion caused Adelaide to feel insecure, she wanted to be informed.

"I was talkin' to them two new fellers over there," Fordy began, nodding toward a nearby table where two cowboys sat working on heaping plates of food Mrs. Morgan had piled high for them.

A few of Mr. Worden's cowboys, as well as Cliff and Boney Bob, sat conversing with the two strangers, and Adelaide smiled, realizing just how entirely fixated on Chance she was to not have noticed new folks in town.

"They're here scoutin' out land for their pa. Seems he wants to start ranchin' somewhere in the county…so I told 'em about our cattle goin' missin'. Figured they oughta know what they're in for."

"Good thinkin', boy," Pop approved. "We don't want someone drivin' his herd out here and losin' half of it to rustlers on the drive."

"Pardon me for intrudin'," Janie's mother, Celia Higginson, said from behind Adelaide.

"Evenin', Celia," Dean greeted with a smile.

"Celia," Pop greeted.

"Mrs. Higginson," Fordy offered.

"Evenin'," Harvey mumbled.

Harvey still had his tail between his legs with lingering embarrassment over being so passionately kissed beneath the mistletoe by the Widow Doyle.

"Merry Christmas, Mrs. Higginson," Adelaide offered, turning in her chair and smiling up at Janie's mother.

"I just had to tell you, Addy, how incredible them sugar cookies of yers are!" Mrs. Higginson sincerely exclaimed. "The ones on the cookie chandelier?"

Adelaide released a light laugh of gratitude and said, "Oh, thank you, Mrs. Higginson! Yer so sweet to take the time to compliment my cookies."

"Oh, you deserve to be complimented on them, sweetie," Janie's mother assured. "They are simply heavenly! In my opinion, they are by far the best tastin' ones on the cookie chandelier—not to mention loveliest lookin' ones! Yer cookie decoratin' skills are the best in Oak Creek."

"Thank you," Adelaide responded, beginning to feel uncomfortable under Mrs. Higginson's gushing.

"And you look so beautiful in this red dress, by the way," Mrs. Higginson added. She bent, placing a tender kiss to Adelaide's temple and patting her shoulder. "Just beautiful!"

"Thank you," Adelaide managed again. She could feel the heat rising to her cheeks. Being that so many folks had praised her beauty that night, Adelaide was certain she'd spent half the time blushing.

"Merry Christmas to you all," Celia said as she took her leave.

"You entered cookies in the cookie chandelier contest this year?" Fordy asked Adelaide.

"I did," Adelaide confessed. "But I never thought they'd be chosen."

"Why not?" Dean asked. "Yer sugar cookies are the best I've ever had in all my life. Stands to reason they'd end up on the chandelier."

"Thank you, Daddy," Adelaide expressed, awkwardly accepting yet another compliment. The fact was, she was plumb worn out from being flattered.

"It's nothin' less than a coup," Pop chuckled. "You've got to be the youngest cookie baker to be chosen for the chandelier, darlin'."

Adelaide giggled as her pop puffed up his chest with pride—and well he should. For although Adelaide was delighted that her cookies had been chosen to join the other winners on the cookie chandelier, she had never expected it. The Oak Creek Christmas cookie chandelier had been a town tradition since her own daddy was a boy. Each year everyone who wanted to participate in the contest presented a plate of five dozen cookies to a panel of judges the day before the Christmas bazaar and dance. Each set of cookies was baked with a small hole punched in the top, just in case chosen for the chandelier. The judges secretly selected three winners and then spent the next morning stringing the winning cookies with thin ribbon ties and attaching them to three wooden frames of three varying sizes that had previously been attached together by lengths of thicker ribbon to form the descending shape of a chandelier. Once the cookies were all hung on the frames, the effect was lovely. Instead of a chandelier composed of glass and prisms, a beautiful chandelier of cookies hung from a specially constructed stand. The Oak Creek Christmas cookie chandelier was always the centerpiece of the desserts table and lent a crowning glory to the rows and rows of sweet things to eat.

Therefore, Adelaide didn't fault her pop's pride in her cookies being chosen for the cookie chandelier. It was indeed an honor—and a memorable one.

"If everyone is finished eatin'," Mrs. Morgan hollered from the center of the room, "let's get these supper tables cleared away so the dancin' can begin!"

Everyone applauded as Mr. Morgan, Plume Ranch's own Ike Wilson, and Andy Fife began playing their fiddles. For her part, Adelaide's heart leapt nearly into her throat with the joyous anticipation that perhaps Chance would ask her'for a dance.

Janie was at Adelaide's side the moment she stood up from her chair. "I'm so excited for the dance!" she giggle-whispered in Adelaide's ear.

"Oh, me too!" Adelaide quietly sighed. She thought again about Chance's hint that she was the prettiest girl in the Christmas barn. Surely it meant he would ask her to dance—and preferably to a waltz. Her heart began to race with mingled anxiety and hope, for she couldn't imagine anything in all the world more blissful than being held in Chance's arms.

Once Chance had assisted in clearing away the supper tables, he glanced to where Adelaide Plume stood conversing with her friend Janie. Oh, but Adelaide looked a vision! Chance smiled to himself as he thought of the joy and amusement on her face as she'd watched Mrs. Doyle give her brother Harvey what for. She was a rare young woman—one who loved God's creatures with all her heart, laughed freely, and didn't seem to care much about conforming to social expectations. Not to mention she really was the prettiest girl in the Christmas barn—the prettiest girl in town, for that matter. Chance liked everything about Adelaide Plume. And as he stood studying her from across the room, he began to wonder if she were indeed old enough to court. After all, her hair was pulled up in a manner similar to the other women of courting age in town. And the red dress she wore—well, it was not a schoolgirl's red dress in any regard. It wasn't as if Adelaide Plume hadn't had Chance's eye, attention, and curiosity since the day he'd arrived at her family's ranch. It was just that something was changed about her. She looked—well, far more mature in age than Chance had been assuming she was. From apparent evidences, the rising knowledge that Adelaide was indeed old enough to court caused Chance's heart to race a bit. Oh, he knew he'd never be allowed court the boss's daughter—being that Dean Plume no doubt wanted his daughter to have suitors who could provide better for her than a cowboy ever could. Chance didn't plan to cowboy forever—but still, he knew most ranchers considered cowboys too unsettled to court their daughters. And yet what would be the harm in asking Adelaide for a dance? Surely Dean and Pop Plume wouldn't fault him for that. It was the Christmas season after all—a time for merriment and fun.

Determined to ask Adelaide for a dance, Chance started toward her when the fiddlers began playing a waltz.

"Chance, honey?"

Chance felt a hand on his arm and looked to see Mrs. Doyle standing next to him. She smiled up at him, and his heart pinched a little in knowing that she was probably not long for the earth.

"Yes, ma'am?" he asked.

"Would you mind givin' an old lady a thrill and dancin' with me?" Mrs. Doyle asked, blushing. "I don't know if I'll have the opportunity again. And I know it just ain't proper, me askin' you to dance, but I—"

"'Twould be me great honor, it would, Mrs. Doyle," Chance said, bowing a little as he took her hand in his.

Admittedly, Chance was disappointed, being that he had hoped to dance with Adelaide. But his heart was so tender where Mrs. Doyle was concerned, and he knew there was no woman more deserving of a Christmas waltz than his sweet friend. Even if she hadn't just done him such a magnificent favor where Harvey Plume was concerned, she held his kindness and affection.

"What fun that was!" Mrs. Doyle laughed, winking at Chance as he took one of her hands in his, placing the other at her waist. "Harvey Plume gets my dander up more than anybody in town," she added. "It was pure joy seein' him squirm like that!"

"Indeed it was, Mrs. Doyle," Chance chuckled in agreement. "And I thank ye far it."

"Oh, don't thank me, honey," she cooed. "That's the most fun I've had in a decade! I'm so glad ya let me in on yer little scheme."

"Aye. I don't know if the man learned anything from it, but it made me own heart happy, it did," Chance confessed. "To my way of thinkin', the man's a two-legged ass, if he's anythin' at all."

"Agreed," Mrs. Doyle stated with a nod. "For the life of me I cannot figure how it's even possible that Harvey Plume come outta that family. I've known Pop Plume since he and his wife moved here…known Dean since he was born. Sweet Adelaide is a jewel, a priceless jewel, and Fordy is the kindest young gentleman a body ever knew. And then there's Harvey." Mrs. Doyle shook her head, exhaling a heavy sigh of exasperation. "It just don't make a lick of sense."

"No, indeed, it doesn't," Chance agreed.

They were quiet for a moment as they waltzed; after all, Chance knew Mrs. Doyle wasn't accustomed to the physical exertion.

Still, after a moment he leaned down closer to Mrs. Doyle's ear and, lowering his voice, asked, "Would ya answer a question for me, love?"

"Of course, darlin'! Anything," Mrs. Doyle assured him.

"How old is Miss Adelaide...exactly?" Chance inquired. "It's a difficult thing far me to determine, it is. Far one minute she's out ridin' her pet bull, hair hangin' free in the wind and not a care in the world it would seem. Then the next minute, she's walkin' into this festive barn, lookin' as if she's ready to be snatched up by the first single man that can snatch her up, she is."

Mrs. Doyle's smile broadened, and she reached out with one soft yet weathered hand and patted his cheek.

"She's a jewel, Chance," Mrs. Doyle answered, "a rare one at that. And she'll be eighteen in just a month or two. So if yer thinkin' about snatchin' her up yer own self...ya best be quick about it."

"Well, I don't know if...I mean to say, I'm not a wealthy man by any means and—" Chance began.

But Mrs. Doyle shook her head, interrupting, "Oh, Adelaide Plume wouldn't look twice at a wealthy man. But a hard-workin' man of integrity, a man who knows her well enough to pull off a plan to give her brother his deserved comeuppance the way you did tonight..." She winked at Chance, continuing, "Now *that's* a man who will win her heart." Chance smiled as Mrs. Doyle added, "If he hasn't already won it."

"She be the boss's daughter, lass," he reminded.

Mrs. Doyle laughed heartily then. "Ah, I haven't been a lass in sixty years, my boy! But I love ya all the more for callin' me one!"

The music ended, and Chance placed his arm around Mrs. Doyle's waist. The dance had worn her out. He knew it had by the perspiration beading on her sweet, wrinkled forehead and her shortness of breath.

"Thank ya for the dance, sunshine," Mrs. Doyle sighed.

"Thank *you*, lassy," Chance offered.

"And now, although I do hate to be a bother," Mrs. Doyle began, "do ya think you could see me home right quick, darlin'? To be honest, I'm a little wrung out and not sure I should make the walk alone…even with my house bein' so close."

"Of course," Chance assured her. "It would be me pleasure and me honor, Mrs. Doyle."

"Thank ya, honey," Mrs. Doyle breathed. "And thank you for such a wonderful evenin', as well. I haven't laughed that hard in years!"

Adelaide watched as Chance helped Mrs. Doyle to sit down in a chair as he retrieved her coat from a hook near one of the barn doors—as he helped her put her coat on, even buttoning the front up for her nice and tight. He was so wonderful! Oh, certainly Adelaide had hoped that Chance would ask *her* to dance the first waltz. But when she'd looked up to see him dancing with Mrs. Doyle—well, her heart had nearly melted with further admiration for him, for his kindness and thoughtfulness to the old lady. And as she watched him assist Mrs. Doyle to standing once more and link her arm with his for support as they started toward the barn door, Adelaide's smile broadened, and tears leapt to her eyes. Chance did not hurry as they walked. Instead, he matched Mrs. Doyle's slow, cane-assisted pace as they left the barn, no doubt heading for her home. Chance Flannery was a rare and wonderful man—whose kindness was sincere, whose striking physical appearance was something out of mythology, and whose sense of humor was as mischievous as Adelaide's.

"He's simply sublime," Adelaide sighed in a blissful whisper.

"Pardon me, ma'am," a man's voice sounded from behind her.

Adelaide turned to see one of the young men apparently searching out property for their father standing behind her. He was very tall, with sandy brown hair and green eyes.

"Might I ask for this dance, miss?" the man asked. "My name's Bill Burlinson, ma'am. And I'm trustworthy, I assure you."

Adelaide glanced to where her father and Pop sat watching folks dance. As if he felt her gaze, her daddy looked to her and nodded his unspoken reassurance that he would keep an eye on her—keep her safe.

"Thank you, Mr. Burlinson. I'd be honored," Adelaide politely accepted. Of course, she wasn't honored, and she didn't want to dance with anyone but Chance. Still, if Mr. Burlinson's family would be moving nearby in the future, Adelaide figured she ought to go ahead and be neighborly from the get-go.

Yet as Mr. Burlinson led her to the dance area in the center of the barn, Adelaide glanced over his shoulder to where Chance and Mrs. Doyle had disappeared into the night. How she hoped he would return soon. And how she prayed he would ask her for a dance—a waltz! St. Nick himself could never bring her a more magnificent gift than waltzing with Chance Flannery—especially if they happened to waltz beneath the mistletoe!

CHAPTER SEVEN

"My brother Fordy tells me you all are here lookin' for land to run cattle?" Adelaide asked Bill Burlinson as they danced. Even though she'd rather be dancing with Chance, she figured it would be wise to get to know a young man who might turn out to be a member of the community.

"Yes indeed," Bill answered. "Me and my brother, Joe, came on out to Oak Creek to scout out the county. Yer brother says yer family's ranch does real well."

Adelaide smiled with pride in her father and grandfather's success. "I suppose so," she said. "And our neighbor Mr. Worden seems happy with his ranch too. So it seems you've chosen a good place to look. Does yer family already raise cattle?"

"Yes, ma'am," Bill affirmed. "I understand yer family runs longhorns."

"We sure do," Adelaide confirmed, her mind wandering to Roger for a moment and hoping he was cozy in his stall.

"Well, we raise Angus as well as Angus bred with longhorns," Bill offered.

"Oh, I've seen Angus!" Adelaide exclaimed. "I think they are just so pretty! And Daddy says they're a fairly new breed in these parts."

Bill nodded. "Very new," he stated. "My pa bought a few bulls 'bout ten years back and bred 'em with longhorns. It made for a hearty herd and good beef."

"Well, I'm interested to see them," Adelaide offered. "I wish you well in findin' the sort of land yer lookin' for. It's always nice to have new neighbors."

"Yes, it is," Bill agreed, smiling at her. "And might I say that this town sure knows how to celebrate Christmas!" He chuckled, adding, "I ain't never seen a barn look so beautiful inside. And the food…well, I ain't had this much good food in one day in all my livin' life."

Adelaide laughed, delighted at the young man's joy. "Oh, I'm glad yer enjoyin' it! It really is one of my favorite things about Oak Creek—the holiday celebrations we have all together as a town."

"Well, it sure does seem like a nice, friendly place," Bill remarked. "I hope me and Joe find some land our pa will approve of."

"Oh, I'm certain that you will," Adelaide encouraged.

Just then Harvey and Janie moved closer during their own waltzing so that they were right next to Adelaide and Bill.

"Hello there, feller," Harvey greeted kindly. "I hear you and yer brother are here lookin' for land to raise cattle on."

"That's right," Bill affirmed. He offered his hand to Harvey, and Harvey grasped it, giving a firm shake. "Bill Burlinson."

"Good to meet you, Bill. I'm Harvey Plume," Harvey offered. "And I see you've already met my little sister, Adelaide, here."

"Yes, sir," Bill said. "Found the courage to ask her for a dance on my first night in town."

Harvey chuckled. "Well, watch out there, Bill. She's as clumsy as a June bug. She might squash yer toes to pulp if yer not careful."

Adelaide glared at her older brother as Janie gently scolded, "Harvey Plume! You be nice to yer sister."

Bill grinned down at Adelaide and said, "Oh, I can't imagine how any lady so pretty as this could ever be anything but graceful."

Harvey laughed—and loudly. "Well, you've been warned, feller. You've been warned." Then he whisked Janie away, leaving Adelaide frustrated and losing confidence.

Still, Bill reassured, "I guess I ain't the only big brother who has trouble admittin' my baby sister is all grown up. You don't pay him no mind, Miss Plume. Big brothers are ornery critters."

Bill's encouragement did lift Adelaide's spirits once more, and she said, "Thank you, Mr. Burlinson. It helps knowin' that there are other big brothers in the world as skunky as Harvey."

Bill smiled and nodded, and they waltzed in silence until the song ended.

"Thank ya for the dance, Miss Plume," Bill said, offering a slight bow.

"Thank *you* for askin' me, Mr. Burlinson," Adelaide countered sincerely. "And I hope you and yer brother find a place out here."

Bill Burlinson nodded, turned, and strode away.

Glancing hopefully at the door though which Chance and Mrs. Doyle had exited, Adelaide's heart sunk when she saw that Chance still hadn't returned.

"Merry Christmas, everyone!" Andy Fife hollered then. Stomping his foot in rhythm, he added, "Turkey in the Straw!"

"Would ya honor me with a dance, baby sister?" Fordy asked, arriving to stand next to Adelaide.

Adelaide giggled, "You bet, big brother!"

Hand in hand, they were off to join the excitement on the dance floor. Adelaide noted that Harvey and Janie were sharing another dance and fought the irksome taste that rose in her mouth. Harvey was not deserving of Janie! Fordy, on the other hand...

"Are you gonna ask Janie for a dance, Fordy?" Adelaide asked her brother.

Fordy shrugged. "If I get around to it," he answered. "I got my eye on that pretty little Sylvia Anderson tonight though."

Adelaide smiled, for Sylvia was indeed a kind and very pretty young lady. A year or so older than Adelaide, Sylvia was quiet and graceful, with blonde hair and blue eyes. Sylvia had always reminded Adelaide of a butterfly for some reason. Now that she knew Fordy was interested in Sylvia, Adelaide felt her heart warm a little—for she could imagine no more perfect wife for Fordy than Sylvia would be.

"Sylvia is an angel, Fordy," Adelaide said to him. "You be sure you dance with her at least twice tonight, all right?"

Fordy frowned a bit. "If I can get to her before Harvey does," he grumbled. "He's already pulled half the girls in town under the mistletoe and slobbered on 'em. I hope he don't get his hands on Sylvia."

"You just be the one to make sure he doesn't," Adelaide instructed. "Besides, if what Janie says is true, Harvey kisses like an old, drooly hound dog. So you best protect Sylvia from that."

Fordy laughed, "I guess I'd better at that!"

Adelaide laughed as they danced a galop quadrille through the remainder of "Turkey in the Straw." And as the fiddlers neared the end the song, Harvey and Janie again appeared, Janie's face beaming with delight and the exertion of the dance. The song ended, and everyone applauded, having had a wonderful dance.

However, as Adelaide clapped, she took a step backward, tripping over something behind her and falling to the floor, landing with a painful thud on the barn floor.

"Harvey Plume!" Janie gasped. "You did that on purpose! I saw you! You tripped Addy on purpose!"

"Oh, I did not," Harvey chuckled, grinning down at Adelaide.

It was Fordy who came to her rescue, helping Adelaide to stand quickly, before too many people had a chance to see her sitting sprattle-legged on the floor in her red dress.

"You really are a jackass, Harvey," Fordy growled, helping Adelaide to her feet.

"Oh, yer as stiff-necked as Pa and Pop, Fordy," Harvey laughed. "It's just a bit of fun."

"Fun for who, Harvey?" Janie asked.

Through the tears of pain and humiliation brimming in her eyes, Adelaide could see the anger and disgust in Janie's. The visual indications that perhaps Janie was finally ready to face the fact that Harvey was a skunk and not worthy of her admiration, let alone her heart, bolstered Adelaide's emotions somewhat.

Chuckling, Harvey looked from Fordy to Janie and then to Adelaide, asking, "Oh, come on. The three of you are a bunch of borin' ol' sticks-in-the-mud. It's Christmastime! Can't a man have a little fun around here?"

"It wasn't fun, Harvey," Fordy growled. "Especially not for Adelaide."

"You know what, Harvey Plume?" Janie asked, glaring up at Harvey.

"What's that, Janie Higginson?" Harvey mocked with a sneer.

"Adelaide's right. You *are* a skunk!" Janie retorted. Janie spun on her heels and began to march away—but not before she turned around once more, adding, "And Fordy's right too! You're a jackass!"

Adelaide's eyes widened at Janie's outburst.

"You really stepped in it this time, Harvey," Fordy said. "If it weren't for the fact we're here celebratin' the comin' of the Lord, I'd lay you out flat for hurtin' Adelaide again. Just know, when we get back to the ranch—"

"Oh, when we get back to the ranch, what, little brother?" Harvey goaded.

Fordy straightened his posture, rolling his shoulders back in a threatening manner—and for the first time, Adelaide realized that Fordy was actually just a hair taller than Harvey. She'd never noticed it before, but it was true. Somewhere along the way, over the past few months, Fordy had edged ahead of Harvey in height.

"You best wait 'til we get home, Fordy," Harvey threatened, "else I'll wipe the floor with you right here in front of everybody in Oak Creek."

Adelaide glanced around to see that many of the folks on the dance floor stood staring at the Plume brothers with unsettled anticipation. Even Ike Wilson and Andy Fife stood with their fiddle bows poised above their fiddles, ready to begin a new tune—but mesmerized to stillness as they stared at Fordy and Harvey squaring off like two ten-point bucks.

"Oh, you could try to wipe the floor with me, Harvey," Fordy began. "But I don't think you'll still be standin' once Pa's finished with you."

"What?" Harvey said, whirling around to look in the direction Fordy nodded.

Adelaide looked as well, pleased as punch when she saw Janie standing with Dean Plume, in obvious tattling on Harvey. Janie looked as mad as an old, wet hen, her hands and arms gesturing this way and that as she talked with Adelaide's daddy.

"She's tattlin' on me?" Harvey's voice squeaked with an intonation two octaves higher than was normal. "And after I treated her so nice this evenin' and all."

Adelaide watched as her father's face grew red with irritation—as he nodded at Janie, even took one of her hands in his, patting it with assurance that something would be done about what had happened. An obviously angry Dean Plume turned toward the place where Adelaide, Fordy, and Harvey stood.

As Dean's long stride brought him nearer and nearer, Fordy mumbled, "See? I won't have to lay you out, brother. Pa's gonna do it for me."

Adelaide almost smiled as she saw Janie remain behind, standing next to Pop, her arms folded across her chest with triumph, as she scowled at Harvey.

"Now, Pa," Harvey began, holding up one hand in a pointless effort to calm his father as he reached them.

But Dean didn't even look at Harvey.

Rather, he reached out, placing a hand on each of Adelaide's shoulders, and with fiery determination in his eyes promised, "This is the last time yer brother will hurt you, Addy darlin'. In any manner."

Adelaide nodded, intimidated by the conviction in her father's countenance.

"Are you all right, sweetheart?" he asked.

"Yes, Daddy," Adelaide assured him.

Then the barely restrained wrath of Dean Plume turned to his eldest son. "Get outside. Now!" he growled in a low, cautionary voice.

"But, Pa—" Harvey began.

"I said now," Dean commanded.

There was no happiness in knowing her brother was about to get, if nothing else, the tongue-lashing of his life—only sadness that her older brother could be so heartless and cruel when it came to her. Certainly, she hoped that this time her daddy's warnings would sink into Harvey's thick skull, that Harvey would quit pestering her so badly. But it still didn't mean she found joy in the contention it would cause.

"You all right, Addy?" Fordy asked, placing a soothing hand on her shoulder.

"Of course I'm all right," she answered, forcing a smile of reassurance as she looked at him. She was so thankful for Fordy—for her kind and loving brother.

"Are you sure?" he inquired once more, visibly unconvinced her answer was wholly honest.

"Yes. I am," she contended. And even though it wasn't all right—even if her sitter hurt worse than it had the week before when Harvey had pulled the chair out from under her—she *would be* all right. Especially if the entire incident caused Janie to finally open her eyes and see what a stinky skunk Harvey really was.

As she watched her daddy and Harvey exit through the barn door through which Chance had disappeared just a short time before, she again prayed that Chance would return soon. She knew nothing would heal her humiliation like a dance with Chance. Still, the handsome cowboy who had unknowingly won her heart did not reappear, and Adelaide exhaled a heavy sigh of discouraged disappointment.

"I swear to you, Addy," Janie began through clenched teeth as she returned, stepping up to stand next to her friend again. "If this wasn't supposed to be Oak Creek's most neighborly, kindest event of the year, I woulda slapped yer brother Harvey right upside the head!"

"I can see that," Adelaide noted, smiling with admiration at her friend's determined temperament.

"I'm not joshin', Addy!" Janie continued to rant. "I hope yer daddy turns that boy over his knee and paddles the livin' daylights outta him!" She looked to Adelaide, frowning. "Yer right; you've been right all along. Harvey *is* a skunk! And furthermore, I bet a skunk could do a better job of kissin' under the mistletoe. I swear kissin' Harvey was not at *all* what I always thought it would be. Good golly, I hope all men don't kiss like they're lickin' an icicle."

"I'm sure they don't," Adelaide consoled her friend. "Otherwise not a woman in the world would get married."

"You sure yer all right, Addy?" Fordy asked.

Addy glanced at her brother to see his gaze following Sylvia Anderson as she used a pair of scissors to cut the ribbon of a cookie on the cookie chandelier.

"Yes, Fordy, I'm fine," she told him. "Now you go get Sylvia Anderson before some other feller does."

Fordy smiled kindly and lovingly at her and then hurried off toward Sylvia.

"I can't believe I wasted all this time—*years* even—moonin' over Harvey!" Janie continued to grumble. "Why, he's nothin' at all like yer daddy! I always thought Harvey might turn out to be like yer daddy...but he sure did not!"

"Nope," Adelaide agreed.

"Oh, I'm as mad as a bull in a barn full of bumble bees!" Janie persisted. She inhaled a deep breath—an understandable attempt to calm herself. Exhaling, she asked, "Do ya want to get some punch to drink?"

"No," Adelaide answered, however. "You go on though. I think I need some fresh air. It's hot in here too."

Janie offered a sympathetic smile, and Adelaide knew she understood her desire to escape the barn for a time. After all, Harvey had taken the fun out of the dance for her, and without Chance there, the fun seemed to have gone out of everything altogether.

"All right," Janie said, exhaling another calming breath. "I'll get myself a cup of punch and cookie off the chandelier. It'll help me to calm my nerves a bit."

"Oh, I'm certain it will," Adelaide said, smiling.

Straightening her posture, Janie added, "Maybe I'll even have two cookies. And maybe I'll find a couple of other girls here tonight who Harvey slobbered all over, and we can commiserate."

"Perfect!" Adelaide giggled.

And as the fiddlers began to play "It Ain't Gonna Rain No More," Janie started toward the table laden with punch bowls, cups, and the cookie chandelier.

Quickly, Adelaide made her way across the room to the door opposite the one her father had ushered Harvey out. She didn't want to hear what was going on between her daddy and brother, for she knew she might burst into tears—especially if Chance happened to return at the same moment. No, Adelaide needed some solace—a little time to work the soreness out of her sitter and her feelings.

The very instant Adelaide stepped out of the barn and into the cold night air, she felt her spirits rise. She saw the silver moonbeams illuminating the dark, leafless trees, the beautiful canvas of cobalt scattered over with glistening, diamond-like stars. It was truly a heavenly night! The warm light from inside the barn shone out onto the ground like pools of liquid gold, and the music wafted over the air, causing nature's beauty to envelop her like a dream.

Adelaide glanced up to the old oak standing nearby, smiling as she wondered how many berries had been plucked from the bunches of mistletoe she and Janie had hung in every doorway and window and from the low center ceiling beam of the big barn. And instead of feeling sad that Chance had not plucked a berry for her under a bouquet of the kissing plant, Adelaide found felicity in knowing that Janie had been kissed by Harvey—and that she had determined she never wanted to be kissed by him again.

"Oh, you are a lovely thing," she whispered, gazing up at the moon—the great and glowing pearl that was the angel's window from heaven to earth. "And you comfort me. No matter what, you comfort me. Whatever would I do without you?"

As Chance hurried toward the big barn, he could hear the sound of voices raised in anger. He knew he should walk around to another entrance, but since he'd neglected to take his own coat when escorting Mrs. Doyle home, he was chilled, and the warmth of the barn was just too alluring to put off, even for another minute or two. Therefore, he figured he would simply avert his gaze—not look directly at the two men arguing just outside of the door.

As he drew closer to the barn, however, he recognized the voice that growled, "One more time, boy—and I mean it—you do somethin' like this one more time, and I don't care if you *are* my own flesh and blood. You can start lookin' for another rancher to work for, you hear me, boy?"

Chance saw that it was Dean Plume who stood wagging an index finger at his son Harvey.

"Oh, come on, Pa," Harvey chuckled. "You don't mean that."

"I do, Harvey," Dean assured his son. "I am sick to death of the way you treat yer sister! It ain't right! And these last two times, ya physically hurt her too. And I ain't gonna stand for it. I wouldn't allow any other man to treat Addy the way you do, and I sure as hell won't allow you to do it! So straighten it up, or I mean it: yer fired. And furthermore, if it happens just one more time, then you can find another place to live too. Yer lucky I don't beat ya bloody and raw for doin' what you did tonight. Fact is, I still might. So wipe that grin off yer face and act like the man I raised ya to be...or you *will* suffer consequences. Understood?"

Harvey nodded, and Dean growled, "I can't hear yer brains rattling, Harvey. Speak up."

"All right, Pa," Harvey mumbled halfheartedly.

"And you start treatin' yer sister like the lady she is—with kind words, manners, and the like. I mean it, boy," Dean added.

"Yes, Pa," Harvey conceded.

Dean straightened his tie and his posture. "Now I'm goin' on back in to have myself a good time. You can go back in as long as you act like a gentleman. If ya think ya need to stew and pout like a child, then go on home."

"Yes, Pa," Harvey sighed.

"Chance," Dean said, nodding toward Chance as he passed the two men.

"Boss," Chance acknowledged just before he stepped into the warmth and merriment of the big barn. He thought for a moment about the cold outside—and not just the temperature but the discourse between father and son—noted what a different atmosphere the warmly lit, food-fragrant, music-bedecked barn held inside. In the same instant, he registered that Harvey "the

96

Skunk" Plume must've pulled another prank on his sister. He frowned, wondering how on earth the idiot didn't swallow enough of his own humiliation tonic when Mrs. Doyle had gone at him with her lickery kisses.

Scanning the dancing couples, searching for Adelaide, Chance scowled as Janie Higginson began striding toward him, wearing her own frown.

"I hope Mr. Plume is beatin' the snot outta Harvey," she grumbled. "You shoulda seen what he did to Adelaide while you were walkin' Mrs. Doyle home, Chance!"

Chance was a bit surprised that Janie Higginson, who had never before said anything other than hello to him, was now standing in front of him telling him what would probably be considered family business to the Plumes.

"Well, there's not snot flyin' about out there," Chance admitted—wishing there had been. "But that idiot Harvey is gettin' a tongue-lashin' and a threatenin' the likes I've never seen."

"Well, believe me, he deserves it!" Adelaide explained. "Adelaide was dancin' with Fordy, and when she was finished, Harvey tripped her, and she went down like a brick! And I know her sitter was still sore from Harvey pullin' that chair out from under her last week."

Something down deep inside Chance soared to consciousness in that moment. Truth was, he'd been fighting his attraction to Adelaide Plume since the first day he'd seen her riding away on her pet steer. But now he knew she was indeed old enough that his attraction to her was justified and proper—not only his attraction but also the ever-present urge to be her protector.

"Well, if his father doesn't beat the blitherin' fool to a bloody paste, I might," Chance growled. "Where be the lass now?"

"Oh, you know Adelaide," Janie sighed. "She's puttin' on indifference about it all. But I saw her slip out the other door a bit ago…and without her coat. I figure she's moon-gazin' again. She does that whenever she's upset."

Chance nodded, mumbling, "Thank ye, Miss Higginson. If you'll excuse me a moment, I'll be lookin' in on her."

"Good," Janie said, a smile spreading across her face.

Chance was still angry as he strode to the other side of the barn, snatching his own coat from one of the coat hooks as he hurried out. Yet his fury because of Harvey Plume's cruel treatment of his little sister began to be bumped aside by instant breathlessness when he saw Adelaide standing beneath the old mistletoe-ravaged oak tree not too far off.

He paused before going to her, momentarily mesmerized by the vision before him. There she stood—Adelaide Plume—the gossamer light of silvered moonbeams streaming down over her as if heaven itself were awed in admiration of her. The red dress she wore—the way the bodice of it almost slipped from her shoulders, causing her soft, porcelain skin to appear ethereal in nature— somehow caused Chance's mouth to water. But Adelaide Plume was not only beautiful; she was also kind and caring, loving to animals and people, with a sense of humor Chance had never seen in a woman. Chance had recognized that her ability to find amusement in life was rare indeed: her delight at his suggestion that Mrs. Doyle kiss Harvey under the mistletoe, her reading a scandalous book out loud to her steer.

As he stood staring at Adelaide cloaked in a gown of red and moonlight, Chance's torso was filled with such feeling, such emotion, that he inhaled a deep breath to calm himself—was surprised when he found that, without his even being aware of it, his hand had moved to cover his heart. And in those moments, he didn't worry about what he did or did not have to offer the boss's daughter as far as property and wages were concerned. He only cared that she had been hurt and humiliated, and he wanted to be the man to comfort her—wanted to be the only man to comfort her ever again.

CHAPTER EIGHT

"Where's yar coat, lass?" Chance asked as he stepped up from behind Adelaide to stand next to her. "It's as cold as the hinges of hell tonight. Ye'll catch yar death out here, ya will."

Adelaide's heart skipped a beat—but not from being startled. It leapt with joy in hearing Chance's voice, seeing him, and knowing he was standing next to her.

"Oh, I'm...I'm just fine," she assured him. "I don't plan on lingerin' too long. But the moon and stars are too beautiful tonight not to be admired. Don't ya think?"

"Aye, lass," Chance agreed. "But yar still gonna freeze without yar coat, ya are."

"I'll be fine," Adelaide reiterated, smiling at him. He was so incredibly handsome—so handsome it took her breath away. And tall! He seemed so much taller there, standing next to her, and she realized that she'd never stood so close to him when he was standing. Most times she saw him walking from a distance, riding his horse, or sitting at the supper table or around the fire. Even when she'd spoken with him inside the big barn earlier that evening—when she'd purchased the beautiful cradle he'd made—she hadn't consciously noted how tall he was. But standing outside with no one else nearby, she was conscious of it—and a mite intimidated by it.

"Well, if yar goin' to be stubborn and dillydally in the cold night air, I must insist ya keep warm somehow," Chance said, removing his coat.

As he placed his heavy coat around her shoulders, Adelaide sighed with the bliss of knowing the mild warmth inside it came from his strong body.

"See there now?" he asked. "Yar warmer already, ya are."

"Y-yes," Adelaide stammered. "I...um...I suppose it is colder than I'd realized. Thank you, Chance."

"It's me pleasure, lass," he said. He looked up into the sky and studied the moon and stars a moment. Inhaling a deep breath and exhaling it slowly, he noted, "Aye, but it is a lovely night to behold."

"Yes, it is," Adelaide sighed with admiration. With Chance standing next to her, the heat of his body warming her in his coat, it was the loveliest night she'd ever known.

"Yar friend Janie tells me that yar brother seems determined to keep wearin' a skunk's skin," Chance offered, looking from the sky to Adelaide. "Am I to understand that he hurt ya again?"

Adelaide blushed with humiliation but shrugged, feigning indifference. "He's just a skunk. And I doubt skunks ever change their ways."

"Well, when I was returnin' from Mrs. Doyle's, I came upon yar father and brother standin' without the big barn, I did," Chance began. "And from what I overheard, yar father...well, I truly do not think ye'll be mistreated by yar brother again."

Adelaide sighed, unconvinced. "Daddy gets onto Harvey every time...but Harvey just continues to exasperate me."

Once more, Chance inhaled a deep breath, exhaling it slowly. It was almost as if he were attempting to keep his temper in check. "I think this time will be different, lass, I do. Very different."

"I hope so," Adelaide sighed. She smiled then, adding, "Because, if the truth be told, my sitter is gettin' sore from sittin' down so hard so often."

Chance repositioned himself, stepped up, and turned to stand facing her. His eyes narrowed as he somewhat growled, "I want ya to slap Harvey if he dares to repeat his bad behavior, Adelaide. Do not let him get away with such treatment of ye."

Chance's voice had such a tone of restrained anger in it that Adelaide felt her eyes widen as she stared up at him. Furthermore, he'd addressed her by her first name, without a *Miss* preceding it—something he'd never done before—and it thrilled her through and through.

"Slap him? You mean…hurt him?" she ventured. "But…but two wrongs don't make a right. Do they?"

"Slappin' Harvey when he does the likes of what he does to ya isn't wrong, lass. It's deserved, and it's a discipline he needs," he explained. "Yar a woman, ya are, and ya should never let any man treat ye with any disrespect. No matter who he is."

Adelaide felt a new smile tugging at the corners of her mouth. "Yer right, Chance," she realized aloud. "Daddy and Pop, Fordy too—they're always tellin' me to give back to Harvey as much as he gives out. Even *you* see that I should. But for some reason…I-I'm a shrinkin' violet when it comes to it. I-I don't know why. Maybe because men don't like women who…well, men prefer shrinkin' violets. And I guess I'm afraid that you…I mean, that men will think I'm too independent, too strong-willed, and—"

"Perhaps some men do prefer a shrinkin' violet," Chance interrupted when she paused. "But only weak men. A strong lad wants a strong lass, he does. I assure ye of that."

Adelaide blushed under his gaze, for even in the low light of the evening, she could see his eyes smoldering with conviction.

"And besides it all, *ya're* no shrinkin' violet, Adelaide Plume," Chance continued. "Ya're kind, and kindness finds difficulty in harsh actions like slappin' a man...even when he most deserves it."

"I think yer the one who's kind here tonight, Chance," Adelaide said. "Kind to me, at least." She burst into giggles as the vision of Mrs. Doyle kissing Harvey under the mistletoe unexpectedly leapt to the forefront of her mind. "Yer scheme where Mrs. Doyle and Harvey were concerned...that in itself was better than a slap to Harvey's skunky face! I truly thought I might burst into laughter and give us away! The look of surprise and embarrassment on his face..." She laughed.

Spurred to amusement by Adelaide's, Chance chuckled, "I've not ever seen a man's face turn such a blazin' shade of red...not in all me livin' life!"

Adelaide tossed her head back, covering her mouth with one hand, beset with giggles. "And that kiss she planted on him—why, it went on and on and on!" she added through her tears of mirth. "Old Mrs. Doyle did not let us down tonight. And Harvey will be rememberin' *that* kiss whenever he sees mistletoe for the rest of his life!"

"Aye!" Chance laughed. "It was a sight that will continue to lighten me heart for years to come, it was!"

As their shared laugh finally subsided, Adelaide reached out, placing a grateful hand on Chance's strong arm—his very strong, solid-as-granite arm. "Thank you for that, Chance," she said. "St.

Nicholas himself couldn't give me anything I'd enjoy more for Christmas than I enjoyed seein' Harvey so flustered and self-conscious tonight. And in front of the whole town, to boot!"

"I'm glad I could give ye such a gift then, lass," Chance said, gifting her a wink and a smile.

"If there's ever anything I can do to properly thank you," Adelaide began, "you just let me know—although I can't think of anything that comes near enough."

"Ya do not owe me yar thanks, Adelaide," Chance assured her. "As I said before, it was as much a pleasure for me to behold as it was far you."

"Well, I don't know about that," Adelaide giggled. "It was pretty much the greatest pleasure I've ever known."

Chance quirked one handsome eyebrow. "That folly with Mrs. Doyle and Harvey is the greatest pleasure ya've ever known?" he asked. "Oh, surely yar exaggeratin' it, lassy."

But as residual amusement caused little spittles of delight to skip through her, Adelaide said, "I'm not! The memory of tonight's goin's-on will bring me pleasure forever."

"Aye, but a lass ought to have more than that to think back on when it comes to pleasurable memories," Chance offered, his voice low and somehow more alluring than it even normally was. "And it doesn't seem right to me that Harvey the Skunk should have his kiss under the mistletoe this evenin' and you and I should not, lass."

Adelaide felt her eyes widen as Chance reached out, taking hold of the lapels of his coat that she wore.

As her heart began to hammer in her chest, he asked, "Unless I missed it whilst I was seein' Mrs. Doyle safely home, ya haven't had *yar* kiss under the mistletoe yet tonight, have ye, lass?"

"W-well, I-I…no, b-but…" Adelaide stammered as Chance's powerful hands fisted the fabric of the coat lapels, slowly pulling her closer to him.

"And I far sure and far certain haven't had me own, I haven't," he continued.

He meant to kiss her. Adelaide knew he did! And although she desired nothing more in all the world—literally desired nothing more than to be kissed by Chance—she began to tremble with anxiety. What if he kissed her and was repulsed by her inexperience—or simply repulsed by her? She wasn't sure she could endure the risk of disgusting him and thereby murdering her dreams of somehow winning his heart.

"B-but there's no…no mistletoe out here," she reminded him, desperate to keep herself from disappointing him. "It's all hangin' in the big barn and…"

Chance smiled, a low chuckle of triumph rumbling in his throat. "Oh, but, lass," he mumbled, "ya've fargotten from whence yar harvest came, ya have."

"What?" Adelaide breathed as Chance bent so that his face hovered just a breath away from hers as she gazed up at him.

"'Twas this very tree I found ya climbin' down from earlier today, it was," he explained in a whisper. "And to me own recollection, there was yet an enormous nest of mistletoe remainin' in its branches once ye had reaped what ye needed. And you and I, lass? Ye and me are standin' directly beneath that enormous cluster of kissin' creeper this moment, we are."

"W-we are?" Adelaide choked, even as euphoria began to envelop her.

"Aye, Adelaide," Chance breathed. "We are."

"B-but…but…but…" Adelaide gasped, still afraid that receiving a kiss from Chance would somehow cause her entire world to crash down around her.

"Furthermore, I'm no weak man…and yar no shrinkin' violet," he stated. "Happy Christmas, lassy," Chance whispered, his lips only a breath away from her own.

"H-happy Chri—"

Adelaide didn't remember what she had meant to say. She didn't feel cold, or even angry with Harvey. In truth, as Chance pressed his lips to hers in a careful, tentative kiss, Adelaide couldn't think of anything but the soft, warm essence of Chance's kiss. She couldn't think of the moon, the stars—didn't know what day it was, let alone where she stood. All that was in her mind in those moments were feelings and sensations of bliss and joy.

She was breathless when the kiss ended, opened her eyes—having been unaware that they had closed—and saw Chance grinning down at her. His eyes were narrowed, smoldering with mischief and something else her foggy mind couldn't identify.

"Aye, hell," he muttered. "A man only lives once, he does."

Adelaide gasped as Chance released the lapels of his coat, gathering her into his arms and kissing her again. This time, however, his kiss, though initially gentle, rapidly intensified, and Adelaide's heart soared from a sense of disbelieving bliss into an immediate and powerful desire she'd never experienced—a desire to return Chance's kiss with a vigor she'd never even imagined before.

And when she felt his lips part—sensed the warm moisture of his mouth—her ravenous yearning mingled with her deepest instincts, and she abandoned her bashful hesitation, melting against the warm strength of his body, allowing herself to bathe in Chance's powerful, consuming kiss, and endeavoring to beguile and please him as thoroughly in return.

Far too soon, Chance broke the seal of their lips, gazing down into her face and in a low voice saying, "Aye, no shrinkin' violet be thee, Adelaide Plume."

Adelaide felt the blush of instant timidity rise to her cheeks. Perhaps she hadn't repulsed him with her kiss—but had she caused him to abhor her with her boldness?

"And thar'll be no blushin' over it, lass," he soothed, caressing her cheek with the back of his hand. "Ya returned what ye were given, just as I hoped ye would." His smile faded just a little as he added, "I am sorry if I took too much liberty with ye."

Adelaide smiled, straightening her posture when he released her, even though she was wildly disappointed that he did.

"No...you didn't," she assured him, still blushing for the fact she had been so accepting and returning of his delicious affections. "I just hope you don't think I'm...I'm..." she stammered, searching for the right words to express her hope that he didn't think her sinful for kissing him the way she had.

"I think yar a fine and rare young woman, lass," he assured with a wink. "Still, I am wonderin'...how many mistletoe berries do ye think I ought to shinny up this tree and pluck away as payment for kissin' ya the way I did beneath it?"

"Oh, I don't think ya need to pluck any at all," Adelaide answered. Smiling, she added, "After all, it's nearly Christmas, so let's just leave it be."

Chance chuckled. "Very well. But now let's get ye back into the barn before the cold settles into ya far good."

Even though she wanted nothing more than to linger outside with Chance beneath the old oak and mistletoe for all of eternity, Adelaide nodded in agreement.

"Happy Christmas then, lassy," Chance said with a wink as they started back to the barn.

"Merry Christmas, Chance," she offered sincerely, thinking there could never in all her life ever be a merrier one. For the warmth and flavor of Chance Flannery's kiss lingered, bathing her in merriment indeed!

As they stepped into the big barn, Adelaide thanked Chance as he removed his coat from around her shoulders, placing it on a coat hook just inside the door.

The moon and stars were indeed beautiful that night, but as the beauty and cheer of the townsfolk of Oak Creek enjoying food, dance, and friendship met Adelaide, warming her heart, she was content to be back inside.

"I hear yar one of the bakin' winners to have had the honor of bein' part of this cookie chandelier contest," Chance said, smiling at her.

Adelaide blushed, delighted but also slightly embarrassed by his knowing about the chandelier. "Yes," she admitted. "I'm very flattered to have been chosen, and Daddy and Pop are bein' ridiculous about it—goin' on and on and on about how my cookies are the tastiest on the chandelier."

Chance smiled, saying, "Well, I would certainly enjoy tastin' one far meself, I would. Perhaps ye would join me far a Christmas cookie and a cup of punch or eggnog."

Adelaide nodded, even as her blush intensified. "I would love a cup of somethin' to drink…though I've had my share of tastin' cookies for a while. I ate so many of my own when I was bakin' them that I was sure I'd have to loosen my corset strings and..."

Adelaide gasped as she realized she'd mentioned something so intimate as her undergarments to Chance.

But to her great relief, Chance simply chuckled, placed his hand at the small of her back to urge her toward the tables laden with sweet things, and said, "Let's be off then...to me tastin' yar winnin' cookies and ye findin' somethin' refreshin' to drink."

Adelaide nodded, thrilled by the feel of his hand at the small of her back. In fact, she instantly missed his touch when they reached the table and he removed his hand in order to pick up one of the pairs of scissors that lay beneath the now nearly empty cookie chandelier.

"I'm guessin' yars be these that are mostly gone already," Chance noted.

"Mm-hmm," Adelaide admitted, allowing just a little pride to rise in her bosom.

"And yars be the prettiest, as well," Chance contended, "with colored icin' and in shapes of Christmas trees?"

"Mm-hmmm," Adelaide sighed, adoring he way his Rs trilled when he said *Christmas*. The word seemed so much more cheerful than usual when he said it.

Adelaide watched as Chance clipped the thin white ribbon attaching one of her Christmas cookies to the chandelier. She held her breath as he took a bite and sighed with approval while enjoying the flavor.

"That, me lass," he began, "is the best cookie I've ever tasted in all me livin' life, it is!"

Adelaide exhaled the breath she'd been holding as relief swept over her. "Oh, I'm so glad! Thank you," she said.

"And now, what are ya feelin' ya want to drink?" Chance asked, moving to where the punch bowls were placed.

"Oh, eggnog for me," she answered. "I just love it! It's the nutmeg in it. I swear I could drink the bowl dry all by myself."

Popping the rest of the cookie into his mouth, Chance proceeded to ladle a cupful of eggnog for Adelaide. Handing it to her, he then ladled out one for himself.

"Hmm," he mumbled once he'd tasted it. "'Tis much better without the rum. I like it as such."

Adelaide giggled. "So do I. The nutmeg is so much tastier."

They stood in silence for a few moments until Adelaide felt Chance nudge her arm with his elbow.

"Look at that, lass," he said in a lowered voice. "Yar brother doesn't seem too worse for the wear."

Adelaide looked in the direction Chance indicated. Near the dance floor, standing under the center ceiling beam of the barn, stood Adelaide's pop and daddy, Fordy, Sylvia Anderson, Harvey, and Janie in conversation with one another.

Frowning, Adelaide quietly groused, "I thought Janie was finished with Harvey."

"Aye, don't ruffle yar feathers yet, lass," Chance encouraged as they watched. "She be talkin' to the other young lady there, not Harvey."

Chance was right. Janie did appear to be speaking with Sylvia. But as Adelaide continued to watch, she saw Harvey tap Janie on one shoulder. As Janie turned to look at him, Harvey the Skunk smiled and pointed up—to where a large bunch of mistletoe hung directly over Janie's head.

"That skunk!" Adelaide grumbled. "How can he possibly have the nerve to…"

Yet as Adelaide continued to watch—as Janie straightened her posture, scowling at Harvey—she gasped as Janie turned from Harvey to Adelaide's daddy, reaching out and taking hold of his tie and pulling him toward her. In the next breath, Adelaide heard Chance chuckle with approval as Janie stood on her tiptoes and planted a long, firm kiss to Dean Plume's lips.

Adelaide felt her eyes widen—heard Chance quietly prod "Carry on there, Miss Higginson! Well done!"—as her daddy wrapped his arms around Janie's waist, shifting the control of the affectionate exchange to himself rather than Janie.

Obviously miffed at Janie's shunning him, Harvey turned on his heels, angrily striding toward the place where several young ladies were standing in watching others dance. Harvey held a hand out to Mary Potter, and she blushed as she placed her hand in his as he led her to the dance floor.

When Adelaide looked back to where the rest of her family was standing, it was in time to see Pop clapping his hands with approval as he chuckled, watching his son and Janie Higginson still kissing under the mistletoe. Fordy was smiling from ear to ear, and Sylvia Anderson was blushing the color of summer radishes.

"Yar dad's a valiant man, he is," Chance chuckled. "Stealin' Janie's kiss from yar skunk brother. I admire him even more than I did a moment ago."

Astonished and unable to completely believe what she was witnessing, Adelaide continued to watch as her father released Janie—as Janie, obviously weak in the knees, stumbled back a step or two, her father taking hold of one of Janie's arms to steady her.

As the fiddlers began to play a waltz then, Adelaide's befuddled attention was finally arrested by something else when she heard

Chance ask, "Would ya do me the honor, Miss Adelaide...of waltzin' with me?"

At once her thoughts—of the fact that she'd just witnessed her dearest friend kissing her father—vanished. Could it be she was about to live another dream come true in dancing with Chance?

Looking to him, she saw that he stood next to her, extending his hand.

"I would be honored, Mr. Flannery," Adelaide accepted as the butterflies in her stomach caused her to feel a bit dizzy with enchantment.

The moment she placed her hand in Chance's strong, warm, callused one, goose bumps began racing over her arms and legs. Merely his touch was enough to cause her knees to feel numb and unsteady. Still, somehow she managed to walk into the midst of the waltzing couples, turn, and face Chance as he placed his free hand at her waist.

Adelaide admired the solid mass of his shoulder as she rested her hand on it, and as he began to lead her in the waltz, she was afraid her blissful state would find her as clumsy as an ox. Thankfully, however, her anxiety was short-lived, for being so near to Chance was euphoric and had the effect of driving any other actuality from her mind. All that persisted in Adelaide's thoughts were musings of how wonderful he was, how perfect his kisses were, how handsome he was, and how completely she owned his attention in those minutes as they danced.

"I've never seen such festivities in a town," Chance said as they waltzed. "This barn and its Christmas trimmin's, the food, the friendly folk, and the lovely company I'm keepin'. Aye, Oak Creek is a place unlike any other, it is."

Adelaide smiled, nodding as she agreed, "I will agree that we come together just dandily this time of year. For every holiday, in fact. But Christmas is our biggest and best gatherin', and I'm so glad you've enjoyed it."

"Aye, I have," Chance confirmed. "And I'm regrettin' that I volunteered to ride the fence line tonight. For it means I must leave once our dance has ended."

Adelaide's heart plummeted to the pit of her stomach with disappointment. Yet for Chance's sake, she sighed with disappointment rather than bursting into tears of sudden distress. After all, the night had held so much more wonder than even she had dreamt. How could she expect more? It would be ungrateful.

"Oh no!" she exclaimed with sympathy. "I'm so sorry you have to leave. But…but I suppose you were able to enjoy the best parts: the food, the company—"

"The mistletoe," Chance added with a mischievous wink.

Adelaide blushed, feeling somewhat too warm suddenly. "Y-yes…the mistletoe."

Chance chuckled, "And I'll never forget the look on yar brother's face when Mrs. Doyle had at him. That memory will keep me merry for a year and a day in the very least, it will."

Adelaide giggled, remembering how wonderful it had been to see Harvey so thoroughly embarrassed. She promised herself then and there to do something very special for Mrs. Doyle.

"I think it will keep me merry in the very least *forever*," she laughed. "That, and the way Janie snubbed him under the mistletoe only minutes ago. I think she has finally seen Harvey for what he really is: a skunk. Thank you so much for schemin' with Mrs. Doyle for me."

"Ah, lass, it was me pleasure," Chance assured her.

They shared lighthearted conversation as they waltzed then, and when the dance had ended and Chance led her back and stood with her near the table where one last cookie hung from the cookie chandelier—a cookie that was not Adelaide's—she sighed with contentment. Adelaide Plume could not have wished for a more perfect evening! Even with Harvey's mean-spirited shenanigans resulting in her sore sitter, she would never wish to change anything about this night. Had Harvey not been a skunk, Adelaide wouldn't have wandered outside to find respite in the beauty of the night. Therefore, Chance would not have had reason to seek her out—to find her standing under the old oak tree—to kiss her in such an intimate manner beneath the mistletoe nested in its branches. And then he'd asked her to dance a waltz, and she'd known that joy, as well. No, there could never have been a more perfect night!

"Thank you for the dance, Chance," she humbly and sincerely offered. "And…and for everything else, as well."

"Thank *you*, lass," Chance countered. "And might I beg one small favor from ye before I take me leave?"

"Of course!" Adelaide chirped, eager to grant him anything he might ask.

Chance looked up, quickly grinning as he winked at her. "There be at least one more berry on that wee shrub hangin' above us. Might I steal one last Christmas kiss from ye, Adelaide Plume?"

Adelaide bit her lip to keep from squealing with glee. "It would be my pleasure, Chance Flannery," she answered.

Chance reached out, cupping her chin in one strong but gentle hand. Bending to her, he pressed her lips with his in a firm, lingering, and wholly intoxicating kiss that caused Adelaide's hair to tingle and her toes to curl tight inside her shoes.

"Happy Christmas, lass," Chance mumbled. She could feel the heat of his breath on her lips as he paused in straightening.

"M-merry Christmas, Chance," she breathed.

She watched him go then—watched him stride away toward the barn door to her right, take his coat off the coat hook, and step out into the night.

"Is there somethin' you might wanna tell yer old grandpa, darlin'?" Pop asked as he appeared to her left.

"Um…uh…I don't know what ya mean," Adelaide stammered, blushing—for it was obvious her grandfather had seen Chance kiss her.

Pop chuckled, placed a loving arm across her shoulders, and in a lowered voice said, "Well, I was just wonderin' why yer standin' here kissin' a cowboy right out in plain public, that's all. Not that I mind…and I do approve of yer choice, honey."

Adelaide giggled nervously, blushed a deeper shade of scarlet, and explained, "Why, because of the mistletoe, Pop…of course! It's hangin' everywhere in this barn. Haven't you noticed?"

Pop smiled and placed a loving kiss to Adelaide's temple. "Well, sweet pea, you must be more gullible than I took ya for. 'Cause there ain't no mistletoe hangin' up right here."

Adelaide looked up, gasping with astonished delight when she saw that her grandpa was indeed correct; there was no mistletoe hanging over her. Chance had kissed her before he'd left, and without the prompting of a "wee shrub" hanging over them!

♥

It was late—rather very early—when Chance finally collapsed into his bed in the bunkhouse. His body ached from riding so late and so long in the cold night air. But he figured there were still five or maybe even six hours left before sunrise—enough time to sleep hard and feel rested when he woke.

He exhaled a sigh of fatigue as he punched his pillow several times, pausing to admire the clean white pillowcase he'd purchased at the Christmas bazaar. Ah, but it was soft as a downy chick, it was! Not to mention lovely with its thread embellishments.

Chance grinned, thinking it amusing that he'd purchased the two pillowcases Adelaide had put for sale at the bazaar near to half the hour before she had purchased the doll cradle he'd made. He'd chosen the set of pillowcases because the flowers embroidered on them reminded him of the buttercups that grew on the green grassy knolls of Ireland. He'd almost forgotten about them, for he'd been such a wee lad when his family had traveled to America. Still, the moment he'd seen the pillowcases, he'd determined to sleep on them for as long as they would last. When Fordy Plume had seen Chance putting them in his saddlebags, he'd mentioned that his sister, Adelaide, had made them, and thus the pillowcases had become more than just comfort to Chance—also a delicate treasure.

As his head rested on his pillow and new soft pillowcase, Chance glanced out the window to the moon and stars drowsing in the dark sky. He grinned, thinking of how beautiful, kind, and enjoyable to be with Adelaide was. He thought of her tossing armfuls of mistletoe down from the branches of the old oak tree—thought of the warmth of her small body bound in his arms when he'd kissed her—the sweet essence of her mouth mingling with his own.

His next thought of Adelaide caused him to chuckle out loud. "Roger. Of all the names for a steer. What a playful wee lass she be."

Cliff groaned in response, "Keep quiet, Flannery. Some of us is tryin' to sleep."

CHAPTER NINE

Christmas Eve dawned cloudy and cold. Yet it was Adelaide's very favorite day of the year, no matter the weather. Adelaide loved the soft, sweet, dreamy feel of Christmas Eve, even more than Christmas Day itself—the inviting aroma of freshly baked breads and pies throughout the house, the warmth of the fire crackling in the hearth, townsfolk dropping by to deliver precious gifts of well-wishes accompanied by a jar of jam or apple butter. And as she sat in the parlor, carefully finishing the little down mattress she'd made for the cradle she'd acquired at the town's Christmas bazaar two days earlier, Adelaide mused over how wonderful it would be for her mother's cherished doll to rest comfortably that Christmas Eve night. Adelaide had sewn a small downy pillow and a warm little quilt the day before; thus the cradle mattress was the final piece of soft luxury needed to ensure a perfect resting place for fragile, beloved Fanny.

Adelaide had delighted in every moment of making the bedding for Fanny. Certainly, she'd enjoyed it because it made her happy to think of the doll finally being out of the trunk at the foot of her bed and able to breathe fresh air at last. Still, what she most enjoyed was the opportunity to reminisce on the time she'd spent with Chance at the Christmas bazaar and dance. Oh, what a glorious night it had been! What wonderful kisses she'd relished while being held warm against Chance's strong body! Their waltz had been intoxicating, but not as intoxicating as his pretending they were standing under mistletoe afterward and kissing her once more before he'd had to leave to ride the fence line. All of it was so marvelous, Adelaide would occasionally find herself wondering if maybe she'd dreamed it instead of truly experiencing it.

But it had not been a dream: it had all been so deliciously real! The fact that she was finishing the doll mattress to fit the cradle Chance had constructed was proof that everything about that night had been real, and Adelaide felt as light as air as she stitched. In fact, she found that if she remained very still, closed her eyes, and concentrated, she could not just well remember but almost feel Chance's warm breath on her cheek—his lips touching hers. It was a memory she would hold as the greatest of her life, no matter what the future brought.

Nevertheless, another memory—a disturbing memory—intruded on her resplendent reverie, and she frowned as she thought of the three more head of cattle gone missing from the herd the night of the dance. Mr. Worden had told Pop just that morning that he was missing five more head as well. The knowledge that both the Plume and Worden ranches had suffered such stiff losses was inexplicably worrisome—as was the evident actuality that bad men, rustlers of some sort, were operating so close.

Although determined to solve the conundrum of who was stealing cattle, Adelaide's father and grandfather had promised that Christmas Eve evening would not be the time. Supper that night would be enjoyed by all the cowboys together with the Plume family—all but Harvey, that was, for Dean Plume was still furious at how badly his eldest son had treated Adelaide at the big barn festivities. Therefore, he'd mandated that Harvey should ride the fence lines until every other cowboy had enjoyed his supper and some singing carols around the piano in the parlor afterward. And although Adelaide felt sorry for Harvey, and even a little guilty at being the reason for his having to miss supper with everyone else on Christmas Eve, her daddy had explained over and over to her that it was necessary if Harvey were ever to turn out to be a good man.

And so, as Adelaide tugged at the final stitch of the little doll mattress, knotting her thread and mumbling to herself, "There we go! All finished," she tried not to worry over Harvey too awful much. Setting aside the tiny mattress, her thread, and her needle, Adelaide sighed with contentment as she studied the beautiful Christmas tree in one corner of the parlor next to the piano. The pine tree her father had cut was beautiful, decorated with glistening strands of extruded silver her grandmother had received from a cousin in Germany more than thirty years before, as well as many beautiful colored-glass ornaments her father had collected for her mother over the years. Adelaide knew that when night fell and the only light in the parlor was from the fire, candles, lamps, and moonlight, the Christmas tree would glow with a mesmerizing radiance. As far back as she could remember, Adelaide had spent hours gazing at the beautiful Christmas tree in the low light of Christmas Eve night. The yearly Christmas tree was one of the most fascinating and soothing sights in all the world.

An unexpected knock at the front door caused Adelaide's smile to broaden and her heart to leap in her bosom. Although she knew Chance was out checking the herd, she hoped that he'd found some reason to come to the house to confer with her daddy or Pop. She hadn't seen him all day long the day before or even for a moment that morning, and her mouth began to water at the thought of being able to gaze into his handsome face at last.

Looking out through the small window in the door, she smiled even though it was Janie who stood on the porch and not Chance. She was, as always, joyful to see her dearest friend.

"Merry Christmas!" Janie happily chirped as Adelaide opened the door to welcome her.

"Merry Christmas!" Adelaide responded with rising merriment as she embraced her friend in a warm greeting. "Come in, come in! It's chilly out, and it's toasty warm inside."

"Thank you," Janie said, stepping into the house. She wiped her feet on the rug just inside as Adelaide closed the door behind her.

"I can't believe it's already Christmas Eve," Adelaide noted with a sigh as the thought began to dampen her joy. "And then it will be a whole 'nother year before—"

"Oh, don't you dare, Addy!" Janie scolded in a giggle. "Don't you dare miss a moment of the joy in missin' it already. And besides, I've brought gifts!"

Determining to do as Janie ordered, Adelaide straightened her posture. "Yer right! This is the happiest day for me all year long, and I won't think beyond it...not yet." She smiled, eyeing the brown paper bag Janie held in one arm and the small flat gift so beautifully wrapped in soft blue calico fabric she held in the other. "And you know you do not need to bring gifts," she reminded her dear friend. "Yer friendship is the greatest gift you could ever give to me."

Janie smiled. "Well, I feel the very same way about yer friendship, Addy. But that doesn't mean I can't give ya this as well."

Offering the calico-wrapped parcel to Adelaide, Janie explained, "This is to you from me. Merry Christmas, darlin'."

"Oh, thank you so much, Janie!" Adelaide exclaimed with delight. "Shall I open it now? Or would ya rather I waited until mornin'?"

Janie laughed. "Oh, don't be silly, Addy! Ya know I'm just on pins and needles wantin' to see if ya like it or not."

"Then let's go into the parlor, and I'll open it this very moment!" Adelaide chirped.

"Can we go into the kitchen instead?" Janie inquired. "I've brought somethin' else, and it's for the kitchen."

"Of course," Addy assured.

As Adelaide hurried into the kitchen, impatient to see what lay beneath the soft calico, Janie prattled, "My Uncle Russ and Aunt Lydia took the train up to spend Christmas, and they arrived just last night—and with two whole bushels of pecans with them. So I brought a sackful for all of you, as well as one of the extra brass nutcrackers my uncle and aunt brought with them."

"Oh, Janie, what a treat!" Adelaide gasped. "I do so love pecans! And they are Daddy's very favorite. He'll be so excited when he sees them."

"I'm so glad!" Janie offered, setting the brown paper bag on the kitchen table. "Do ya have a bowl we could put some in? Then they'll be right here on the table whenever you have a hankerin' to have one."

"Yes," Adelaide assured her friend. Quickly she went to the cupboard and removed a medium-sized bowl.

"Perfect!" Janie giggled as Adelaide set the bowl in the center of the table. Opening the brown bag, Janie reached in, gathering a handful of pecans and dumping them into the bowl. As she continued to fill the bowl with the precious nuts, she said, "I'm hopin' these will add a little somethin' special to yer festivities tonight and tomorrow."

"Oh, indeed they will," Adelaide affirmed.

As Janie handed the brass nutcracker she'd brought to Adelaide, she asked, "Did ya get the beddin' finished for Fanny's cradle yet?"

"Just a moment before you arrived," Adelaide answered. Carefully choosing a pecan from the bowl, Adelaide used the nutcracker to crack it open, revealing the tasty meat inside. She pried the pecan meat out of its shell, popping it into her mouth and sighing, "Mmmmm! It's so delicious, Janie. How can I ever thank you? Oh, what a wonderful and very special gift. Thank you!"

Janie smiled with contentment, sighing with satisfaction. "I'm so very glad you like them, Addy." Nodding toward the calico-wrapped parcel Adelaide had laid on the table in order to crack a pecan, Janie urged, "Now open that one. It's not much, but I thought of you every minute I was workin' on it!"

Her heart warmed by Janie's love and friendship, Adelaide retrieved the gift, unfolding the calico to reveal a beautiful white half apron, delicately embroidered with pink roses and green rose vines.

"Oh, Janie!" Adelaide gasped in awe as she held the apron up before her in admiring its delicate beauty. "Janie, it's far too lovely to use for everyday kitchen work! How would I ever feel happy in soiling it?"

Janie giggled, "It's an apron, Adelaide! It's meant to be soiled. And I'm so pleased ya like it."

"Like it? Why, it's the most beautiful apron I've ever seen. Ever! Oh, thank you—thank you!" Adelaide gushed with sincerity. "And it's so much prettier than what I have for you."

"Oh, ya don't have to give me anything, Addy," Janie said. "I just made this for you because—"

But as Adelaide held up one index finger in gesturing that Janie should hush, Janie giggled, watching as Adelaide hurried into the parlor, returning with two white cotton pillowcases, lovingly folded and tied with a green ribbon.

"I made these for you, my sweet," Adelaide explained, holding the pillowcases out toward Janie.

"Oh, Addy!" Janie breathed, accepting them. Untying the ribbon that held them, Janie's smile broadened as she admired the beautiful pillowcases, the cuffs embellished with embroidered pink and yellow honeysuckle and green vines. "They're beautiful. Perfectly beautiful!"

"I hope you like them, Janie," Adelaide said. "I figured, now that you've moved beyond my skunky brother...well, that when you *do* find the man truly worthy of yer heart, then these will be put to good use."

"Thank you, Addy," Janie enthused. "Oh, I just love them! I was hopin' to have a set of yer lovely pillowcases one day."

"You're welcome," Adelaide said, returning her friend's thankful embrace.

"And yer right," Janie sighed, straightening her posture once more. "I am completely over the hill about Harvey Plume! His behavior at the Christmas bazaar and dance was entirely heinous. I could not believe how quickly I went from admirin' him and fawnin' after him like a fresh calf to feelin' abhorence when I looked at him!" Janie shook her head. "What on earth was I thinkin' all these years?"

Adelaide exhaled a deep sigh of relief. Janie had truly gotten over Harvey—at last.

"And I'll tell ya somethin' more," Janie continued. "That slobbery, hound-dog kiss he slathered me with...well, my stomach churns every time I think of it. Bleck! Thank heaven yer daddy didn't kiss me like that when I kissed him under the mistletoe. Otherwise I'd be ruined for life—I swear it!"

Adelaide grinned, her curiosity suddenly piqued about something she hadn't had the chance to discuss with Janie, as they had not seen each other for the two days since the Christmas festivities in town.

"And that reminds me, Jane Higginson," Adelaide began, "I'm guessin' my daddy didn't slobber all over you like an old hound dog, hmmm?"

Instantly a slight blush rose to Janie's lovely face. "Oh no, indeed, he did not," Janie assured with a sigh. "In fact, it was yer daddy that hauled me on over that hill where Harvey was concerned...for kissin' yer daddy was such bliss that it downright knocked some sense into me."

"Do tell?" Adelaide prodded, desperate to hear more about Janie's change of heart toward Harvey—*and* the fact that her daddy was obviously a skilled kisser.

"Well," Janie began, pulling a chair out from the table and taking a seat, "I can't really explain...not the true depth of it anyway," she continued as Adelaide sat down in the chair next to her. "It's just that, when Harvey kissed me, I swear I thought I would throw up right there in the big barn, all over that beautiful Christmas décor we all worked so hard on. But when yer daddy kissed me back—ya know, after I kissed him 'cause he was standin' under the mistletoe and I certainly did not want to kiss Harvey again—when yer daddy kissed me, I swear I thought I might swoon dead away from the deliciousness of it! My knees went weak; I couldn't breathe! I swear there were colors goin' off in my mind that were brighter than the fireworks at last year's Independence Day celebration in town!"

"And did yer toes just squinch up in yer shoes? Did yer hair tingle all over yer head?" Adelaide inquired.

"Why, indeed they did! All of that!" Janie assured her. Janie paused, arching one eyebrow with understanding. "I suppose yers did just that when Chance kissed you after the waltz you two shared."

"Oh, undeniably!" Adelaide giggled. "Just as before we waltzed...when he kissed me outside under the big ol' oak!"

"What?" Janie gasped. "We cannot ever, ever, ever again go two whole days without seein' one another and visitin' over things, Addy! So much has happened, and here we are with hardly any time at all to talk it over, 'cause Mama wants me back home lickety-split! So just tell me the most wonderful parts as fast as you can before—"

The kitchen door opened then, and Dean Plume greeted, "Good afternoon, ladies," as he entered.

"Afternoon, Mr. Plume," Janie responded, blushing so red Adelaide was certain her head would catch fire.

"Hello, Daddy," Adelaide offered. "What brings you in so early today? Are ya hungry?"

"A bit," Dean admitted. He went to the sink, working the pump until a good stream of water began to pour out. As he washed his hands, he said, "But I thought I'd come in and get the gifts of the men lined up. I want to make sure their silver dollars are as shiny as they can be 'fore I give 'em out tonight."

"Oh, I could do that for ya, Daddy," Adelaide offered.

"No, no, darlin'," her father countered, however. "I like to do it. And it'll give me some time to sit in reflection on the meanin' of tomorrow."

"Well, hungry or not, Mr. Plume, you *must* try some of the pecans my uncle and aunt brought to us for Christmas," Janie suggested. "We find them to be quite a treat, so I just had to bring some over to yer family."

"Well, that is awful kind of ya, Janie," Dean said, pulling a dishtowel from the cupboard drawer near the sink. "Awful kind, indeed."

Then, as Dean turned around, his gaze falling to the bowl of pecans on the table, he continued to dry his hands with the dishtowel—a very familiar-looking dishtowel.

"Daddy, did you purchase that dishtowel at the Christmas bazaar?" Adelaide asked. She glanced to Janie, whose blush had turned pure crimson.

"I sure did," Dean confirmed. "I saw it there on the table, and it just looked so nice and soft with all that needlework around the edge that I just had to have it." He smiled at Janie, adding, "Then when Mrs. Morgan told me that you yerself had done 'em up, Janie…well, I knew they were meant for me and mine."

Dean added a wink and a nod to Janie as she stammered, "W-well…well, I do hope you enjoy them, Mr. Plume."

"Oh, I have no doubt that I will, Janie," Dean Plume assured the young woman.

Now it was Adelaide who quirked one brow. Her daddy hadn't purchased Adelaide's pillowcases the way he did every year for fear no one would buy them and her feelings would be hurt. Instead, he'd chosen Janie's tatted dishtowel, and Adelaide was glad for so many reasons. First of all, she knew her father and Pop each had a drawer full of pillowcases embroidered by Adelaide—far too many for two old widowers to ever have use for. But most of all, Adelaide was intrigued with the fact that her father had purchased Janie's dishtowel—that he stood before them both, grinning like Lewis Carroll's Cheshire cat. Still, she shook her head, scolding herself for even beginning to imagine such nonsense as her father and Janie being sweet on one another.

"Um…Mr. Plume," Janie began, "I…um…I overhead my daddy and my Uncle Russ talking last evenin', sayin' that you and Mr. Worden both have had more cattle gone missin'. Are we all in any danger? I mean, with thievin' rustlers and such about?"

"Oh, I don't think anybody is in danger, Janie," Dean soothed, offering a reassuring smile to both Janie and Adelaide. "Not people anyway. Just cows."

Janie exhaled a sigh of relief, but Adelaide's spirits dropped. It was Christmas Eve! She didn't want to think about the fact that cattle rustlers even existed in the world, let alone that a band of them might be operating so close by—stealing her family's cattle as well as Mr. Worden's. Still, she knew cattle rustlers were the only reason so many cattle would go missing. And she also knew that her Daddy, Pop, Mr. Worden, and every cowboy that worked at either ranch were on edge and very wary every moment of the day of late.

"Well, I'm certainly glad to hear that," Janie admitted. "After all, it is Christmas Eve, and with tomorrow bein' Christmas day, nobody wants to be worryin' about rustlers."

"Indeed, they do not," Dean agreed. "So you just enjoy yer family and the goin's-on you all might have planned, and let us cowboys worry about the rustlers, hmm?"

Janie giggled. "I am determined to try, in the very least," she confirmed. She exhaled a sigh of something akin to disappointment, adding, "And I suppose I should be gettin' on home so I can help Mama with supper and all." She looked to Adelaide, placing a friendly hand over one of hers. "I do so love the pillowcases, Addy!" she expressed sincerely.

"I'm so glad," Adelaide said. "And thank you for the beautiful apron, Janie! I promise I'll try my best to find the courage to wear it and risk spoilin' its unsoiled beauty."

"Oh, good gravy, Addy!" Janie laughed. "It's meant to be soiled, silly goose. I best see you wearin' it next time I come in for a visit."

"All right," Adelaide giggled.

"Did ya ride over or walk today, Janie?" Dean inquired.

"I rode ol' Rufus over, Mr. Plume," Janie answered. "He needed a nice Christmas Eve outin'. My daddy has pretty much put him out to pasture, but the ol' boy had a twinkle in his eye when I saddled him up today."

Dean nodded. "Ol' Rufus, huh? Why, he's got to be, what…pert'n near twenty-five years old by now."

"Twenty-six," Janie confirmed.

"I remember when yer daddy bought ol' Rufus," Dean reminisced. "I was near to sixteen that summer, I think. How time does fly."

"And speakin' of time," Janie said, rising from her chair. "I best be gettin' home, Addy."

Adelaide stood, embracing her friend with affection.

"Thank you so much, Janie," Adelaide reiterated. "And Merry Christmas!"

"Merry Christmas!" Janie giggled.

"I'll see you and ol' Rufus home today, Janie," Dean said. Using the brass nutcracker, he cracked open a pecan with flawless skill, tossing the nutmeat into his mouth. "Mmm! I do love these little devils!"

"Oh, I'm so glad, Mr. Plume," Janie chirped. "And thank you for offerin' to see me home. Yer always such a gentleman about makin' sure I arrive at home safe and sound."

Adelaide quirked one eyebrow. Every time Dean or Pop Plume insisted someone see Janie safely home, Janie argued, assuring everyone that it wasn't necessary. And yet as Adelaide watched her father stride forward, place his hand at the small of Janie's back, and direct her toward the kitchen door to exit the house, Jane Higginson did not protest—not a whisper.

"Bye, Janie," Adelaide called as her father and Janie left the house.

"Bye-bye, Addy," Janie called over her shoulder as she and Dean stepped out onto the back porch.

Adelaide felt her smile broaden. Could it be that, in the course of just a few days, Jane Higginson had not only realized what a skunk Harvey Plume was but also transferred her affectionate interests to his father? She giggled, delighted in knowing Harvey would nearly drop dead of astonishment if it happened to be true.

"Oh! Roger!" Adelaide gasped. "I've got so much to do before supper."

Hurriedly, Adelaide went to the parlor, retrieving the copy of Mr. Moore's "A Visit from St. Nicholas" and her warmest shawl. Bustling back to the kitchen then, she gathered six beautifully iced Christmas cookies and headed out the kitchen door and toward the barn.

With all there was still to prepare for the evening's special supper and festivities, Adelaide wanted to wish Roger a merry Christmas and indulge him in their annual Christmas Eve tradition together—the reading of "A Visit from St. Nicholas" and the enjoyment of Christmas cookies. Therefore, although Adelaide usually visited Roger after Christmas Eve supper and the following festivities, she had determined that there might now be someone she wanted to linger with on Christmas Eve more than Roger—Chance Flannery. Of course, Chance may not want or be able to linger for long afterward, but just in case he chose to or were able, Adelaide wanted to make certain Roger was not neglected, for she knew it would break the young steer's heart, as well as her own if he were—especially on Christmas Eve.

"'He sprang to his sleigh, to his team gave a whistle,'" Adelaide read. Taking a bite of the last Christmas cookie she'd brought to the barn, she continued, "'And away they all flew like the down of a thistle. But I heard him exclaim, ere he drove out of sight, Happy Christmas to all, and to all a good-night.'"

Closing the cherished book, Adelaide sighed with contentment as she took another bite of her cookie. She closed her eyes for a moment where she lay against Roger's side in the fresh straw of his stall. She relished the smell of the barn—the clean straw, oats, wood—and the peaceful quiet with only the sound of Roger's low, contented breathing. The air was cold outside, but in Roger's stall all was warm and calm and cozy.

"Here ya go, boy," Adelaide said, sitting up and offering the rest of her cookie to Roger. "I shouldn't be feedin' these to you at all, ya know, but it *is* Christmas Eve, and you deserve to have as much delight as everyone else. Yes, you do."

Roger sighed with agreement, and Adelaide stroked the soft bridge of his nose. She was so grateful her father had allowed her to nurse the poor little steer who had been so badly hurt instead of putting him down—thankful that Roger's terrible wounds had healed and that he had known triumph over adversity and been loved. In those tender moments on Christmas Eve, Adelaide's eyes brimmed with tears as she sat in wonderment at her sweet Roger. What a blessed gift he was.

She was only mildly startled when she heard the barn door open—heard someone's heavy footsteps entering. The stalls where the cowboys quartered their horses were in the barn with Roger's stall. Each stall had a cupboard next to it for storing a saddle, bridle, bit, and other tack. Adelaide figured that one of the cowboys was heading into the barn to ready up for a shift at riding the fence line.

However, when she saw which cowboy had entered the barn, her heart leapt. Chance! Adelaide sat up straight, intending to stand and greet him. Yet one actuality gave her pause: the fact that Chance Flannery wore only trousers and boots. The man had not one other stitch of clothing about him! He wasn't wearing a shirt, wasn't even wearing any sort of undergarment to cover his torso—not a scrap!

As Adelaide's eyes widened in awed astonishment, she was struck not only mute but also breathless. Watching as Chance went to the cupboard housing his rig, she could only stare, stunned into a paralyzed state of admiration by the smooth contours of his muscular shoulders, arms, and chest. She watched Chance frown as he pulled his saddlebags from the cupboard, digging through first one and then the other.

"Dammit," he grumbled. "Where did ye put that flannel shirt, Chance Flannery?"

All at once, Adelaide felt the fool. How ridiculous would she appear when Chance turned to exit the barn and saw her sitting in the straw next to Roger, watching him? Coming upon her reading *The Picture of Dorian Gray* would seem like nothing scandalous at all compared with the possibility of his turning to see her staring at him, mouth agape, as he stood there half naked!

Leaping to her feet, determined to appear unaffected by his scandalous, albeit fascinating state of undress, Adelaide blurted, "Have you misplaced somethin', Chance?"

Chance startled, obviously having thought he was alone in the barn. Still, an alluring, truly seductive smile spread across his handsome face as he answered, "Indeed, it would appear that I have, lass."

"Oh, well...I'm so sorry," Adelaide stammered. She found it impossible to keep from staring at him—impossible not to notice the muscles across his stomach, the way the muscles in his arms tightened as he put the saddlebags back in the cupboard. Oh, she'd seen men discard their shirts before—when the heat of summer was too much to bear or when bath time was at hand. But she had never, not in all her life, seen anything the like of the chiseled, granite-like musculature of Chance Flannery!

"It's not yar fault, Adelaide," Chance assured her with a chuckle. "Not unless ya've stolen me best blue flannel shirt far some unknown purpose. I have the first bout of ridin' the fence line after supper this evenin', I do, and that blue flannel keeps me as warm as toasted chestnuts."

"Oh, I see," Adelaide ventured. "Well, *I* have not absconded with it, I assure you." Although she smiled at the thought of having done so—having secretly taken the shirt so that she might hold it to her face and breathe in the scent of him at her leisure.

"It's certain I stuffed it somewhere else, I did," Chance commented.

As he turned to her and began striding to where she stood in Roger's stall, Adelaide took a step back, nearly stepping on Roger's tender nose where his head lay behind her in the straw.

"And how fares yar Christmas Eve thus far, lassy?" Chance asked, stopping just outside of Roger's stall. "It seems as if I've not had the blessed gift of settin' eyes on ye in a month of Sundays. Are ye enjoyin' yarself? Surely ya've kept busy preparin' for this evenin' and the fancy supper ya're treatin' us dusty cowboys to, hmm?"

"Oh yes, I have," Adelaide confirmed.

Chance offered his hand to her, and she took hold of it, stepping out of Roger's stall and pulling the gate closed behind her.

"I hope it's enough to make yer Christmas Eve a special one," she confessed.

Chance smiled, his eyes narrowing as they began to rather smolder. Adelaide had never seen blue smolder before. Certainly the sky was bright, but it did not smolder as Chance's eyes did in that moment. Adelaide found the essence of it enrapturing.

"Oh, just comin' upon ye so unexpected this way has made this Christmas Eve a vastly special one, lass," he flirted.

Adelaide shook her head a little, trying to cool the blush that had begun to rise to her cheeks when he'd taken her hand. It had grown hot and uncomfortable at his words.

"Do ya know somethin', Adelaide Plume?" Chance asked as he pulled her forward, taking her waist with his free hand, his other remaining occupied in holding hers.

"I know some things, Chance," she teased, giggling. "But I'm not quite sure to which thing yer referrin' to just now."

Chance's smile broadened as he began to lead Adelaide in a waltz, there in the barn, right in front of Roger's stall.

"Aye, ya are a wit, lass," Chance chuckled. "But the thing I'm speakin' of now is that I've never know such regret as I have since the night of the Christmas dance…regret that ye and me had only one waltz."

"Me too," Adelaide confessed, following his lead.

"'*I loved a young lass with eyes like the sea, and hair as black as a pearl,*'" Chance began to quietly sing. "'*She donned a worn dress as green as the hills, that blue-eyed Irish girl. I took her a-walkin' out under the moon, one night when the stars were agleam. And that's where I kissed her, confessin' the truth, that I did her most esteem.*'"

Adelaide bit her lip with delight, for Chance's low, flawless singing voice was as nothing she'd ever before heard—bewitching.

"'*Her lips were as soft and as pink as the rose as she kissed me there under the moon,*'" he continued. "'*And there 'neath the stars we declared our true love and vowed we would marry in June.*'"

Adelaide sighed, entirely mesmerized by Chance—by his voice, the warmth of the flesh of his shoulder as her hand rested upon it.

"Yar grinnin' like an oyster, ya are. Does me singin' pain yar ears, lass?" he chuckled.

"No!" Adelaide exclaimed, breathlessly. "Your voice is like rich, soft cake, or some such delicious thing. And the song is…it's so lovely! So charmin'! Please don't stop. I know there must be more to the song."

"Aye, there be more, Adelaide," Chance confirmed.

Even so, he slowed their waltz until they weren't dancing at all but simply standing there in the barn gazing at one another.

"But it's comin' to me mind…that why would I be wastin' me time singin' about some other lad kissin' his own lass, when I could be kissin' ye, here and now?" he asked in a low, alluring voice that caused Adelaide to step closer to him—to take her hand from his that held it and place it on his shoulder opposite of the one where her other hand already rested.

"Aye," Adelaide breathed, as both his hands settled at her waist, drawing her body flush with his own.

As Chance pressed his lips to hers, gently at first, Adelaide felt her body relax full against his. His skin was so warm she could feel the heat of it through her bodice, and it was an intoxication that nearly sent her swooning. And yet, in the next moment, Adelaide was ever so glad she managed not to swoon, for as Chance pulled her tight against him, his strong, muscular arms banding around her possessively, his kiss deepened, just as it had under the old oak—and Adelaide surrendered any inhibition that remained in her.

Chance's consummate and ambitious kiss worked to coax Adelaide's into a blending of magnificent affection, and she felt as if she had somehow been whisked away from winter, far ahead into the heat of summer. There was nothing about her that was cold, chilled, even the least bit cool. Her toes were warm, her knees were warm, and the sensation of having just eaten sweet summer honeycomb filled every part of her.

Breaking the seal of their mouths for a moment, Chance gazed down into Adelaide's eyes, mumbling, "I will never have me fill of yar kisses, lass. Aye, yar mouth is more delicious than anythin' I have ever in all me life tasted." He winked at her, grinning and adding, "But come tomorrow, when all yar work for Christmas day is done, I think ye and me should find a quiet spot far talkin', I do. So much has happened between us, and we've nary had a breath to sort it out with one another. Would ye find the time to ride out with me tomorrow perhaps? Far yar father has given all we lads the day off for restin'."

"Of course," Adelaide whispered, smiling up at the man she wished she would never have to leave again, not even for one single moment. "There is nothin' I would rather do or that would make me happier than to ride out with you on Christmas Day."

"Let's have one more kiss between us then, to see us through 'til tomorrow," Chance breathed as his mouth descended to Adelaide's once more. "Happy Christmas, Adelaide Plume," he mumbled against her mouth.

"Merry Christmas, Chance Flann—"

But Adelaide's words were lost to the bliss of knowing the warm moisture of Chance's mouth taking hers once more—lost to the feel of his heated skin beneath her palms and to the scents of leather and fresh, chilled air that clung to his face.

The men had eaten more than their fill of the near lavish Christmas Eve supper Adelaide had provided. Seeing the men—especially Chance, her daddy, and Pop—so thoroughly and sincerely enjoying every bite of baked ham, warm bread, fried apples, potatoes, and onions, and every other delectable morsel she had prepared had gifted Adelaide such glorious, Christmas Eve joy that she thought nothing could surpass it. And still afterward, as she sat at the piano playing carols as the men all raised their voices in happy song, the true wonder of Chance's singing voice wafted through her like a garland of gold. He'd sung softly when they'd waltzed in the barn. But around the piano, he joined with the others in bold singing, and Adelaide knew she would never forget the sound of those cherished carols passing from Chance's gifted throat out into the parlor.

Thus, as she lay in her bed, gazing out her bedroom window at the full moon and glistening stars beyond, Chance's voice echoed in her mind—just as perfectly as the bliss of his kiss lingered on her lips. And tomorrow they would ride out together, just the two of them, to talk, to be together without anyone else nearby—even dear Roger.

Rolling to her side, Adelaide leaned over, gazing lovingly at Fanny where she slept in her new cradle, warm and snug in her new bedding. Oh, she knew most folks would find her whim of pampering her mother's doll in such a manner purely foolhardy and silly. But Adelaide cared little for the opinions of others. With the exception of Chance, her daddy, Pop, Fordy, and Janie, she didn't consider too much what others may think of her having a doll in a cradle in her room when she was no more a child than her pop was.

And so tucking the little quilt she'd made more tightly around Fanny's body, Adelaide whispered, "Merry Christmas, Fanny. Sleep tight for me, will you? For I've never slept a wink on Christmas Eve before, and goodness knows, with Chance just across the way in the bunkhouse, I'm bound to lie awake all night long. Nope, it's not the anticipation of St. Nicholas's visit this year that will find me sleepless, dear Fanny." Adelaide paused, giggling. "Although I do wonder when Daddy will realize it is not necessary for St. Nicholas to visit me any longer." Exhaling a sigh of perfect joy and contentment then, Adelaide continued, "No indeed. I'll be sleepless tonight all for not wantin' to wait the hours that I must wait in order to be with Chance again. Oh, Fanny! What a wonderful Christmas Day it will be!"

Adelaide rolled over in her bed then, fluffing her pillow.

And though she knew sleep would be elusive, she closed her eyes, smiling as she quietly sang, "'Her *lips were as soft and as pink as the rose as she kissed me there under the moon. And there 'neath the stars we declared our true love and vowed we would marry in June.*'" Smiling, Adelaide whispered, "Oh, what a lovely song, Fanny. What a lovely song indeed."

CHAPTER TEN

Christmas morning dawned crisp and clear, bright and beautiful. Indeed, snow had fallen during the night but only enough to cover everything with a white and frosted glimmer. Adelaide smiled, closing her eyes and inhaling the fresh enchantment of a cold but still winter's morn. Georgie's and Paddy's hooves crunched the snow and frost beneath them as they lazily walked on, and Adelaide thought the sound was most soothing.

"Aye, what a mornin' it be, lass," Chance remarked, inhaling a deep breath of refreshing atmosphere himself. "Crisp as an icicle yet as sunny as heaven itself, but with just enough snow to honor Christmas Day."

Adelaide nodded, her heart quickening with delight at the sound of Chance's trilled "r" of *crrrisp*.

"It's perfect!" she sighed with admiration of the day—and the man. "I was so glad to wake up to the snow and yet calm air. Otherwise we may not have been able to ride out this mornin'."

"'Tis true," Chance agreed. "And bein' that there aren't many mornin's a hand like me has free, I'm grateful that yar father and Pop gave us cowboys the day off." He paused, his handsome brow puckering slightly, however. "Though I do feel badly that they're ridin' so long themselves, I do. It doesn't seem right, somehow."

Adelaide smiled, her heart further warmed by Chance's concern for Pop, her father, Harvey, and Fordy. Chance Flannery was a thoughtful and empathetic man—traits that made him even more attractive, if such a thing were even possible.

"Our family has always done that—ridden out to do the chores that need doin' on Christmas Day," Adelaide explained. "It is a gift of time to the men who work so hard all year long with us."

"Well, for my way of thinkin', the shiny silver dollars given to us last night is far more than gift enough," Chance noted. He looked over to Adelaide, smiling and offering a wink. "Ya come from a uniquely good family, ya do, Adelaide."

"I think so too," Adelaide agreed.

"Still, it's too bad yar da and all have to ride the fence lines on Christmas Day, it is," he commented. "But yar pop says we'll spend tomorrow trackin' these thieves down, far once and far all. Nobody's gettin' a wink of sleep in the bunkhouse, so I know the same is true for ye and yars in the house."

Adelaide's pretty brows puckered, and Chance knew he'd said too much concerning the matter. Silently scolding himself for returning worry to her mind, he changed the course of their conversation to something else—beginning with what he'd seen the day before.

"I saw yar father ridin' out with yar friend Janie last afternoon," he began.

Chance adored the pink of excitement that rose to Adelaide's soft cheeks, and he thought of how desperately he wanted to caress them in that very moment—in every moment.

"Yes," Adelaide giggled with obvious delight. "She rode over to deliver a gift to me and some pecans her uncle and aunt brought to her family. Usually Daddy has Fordy escort Janie home." She frowned the cutest frown Chance had ever seen and explained, "Bein' that Harvey is a skunk and doesn't deserve to be given the time of day by Janie." Her cute frown disappeared, and the pink of felicity rose to her cheeks once more. "But yesterday, Daddy saw her home. It was almost as if…as if…"

"As if yar da is sweet on the lass?" Chance ventured.

"Yes!" Adelaide exclaimed with obvious glee at the possibility. "*And* I discovered only yesterday that Daddy purchased the tatted towel Janie had made for the Christmas bazaar! He knew it was hers, and so he bought it! Isn't *that* intriguin'?"

Chance chuckled, enchanted by Adelaide's visible joy.

"Aye," he answered. "Very intriguin', indeed."

He watched as Adelaide exhaled a sigh of contentment. "Wouldn't it be wonderful if Daddy…? But then again, folks might think unkindly of Daddy courtin' Janie—you know, because he's so much older. After all, he's old enough to be her…her…"

"Her father?" Chance offered with an understanding smile.

"Yes," she responded.

As Chance watched the joy begin to drain from the young woman he'd fallen in love with, he offered, "Do not worry yar pretty head, lassy. It matters not what people think in such situations as this. And it is far more commonplace for a man to marry a woman much younger than himself, it is. Me own da is thirty years the senior to me mother, and they are as happy as ever they were."

"Truly? Thirty years older?" Adelaide inquired, her beautiful emerald eyes wide with astonishment.

"'Tis true," Chance affirmed. "Me da had also been married before, like yar father was to yar mother. I have me four older half-siblings, three sisters and a brother, as well as two brothers that are me da and mother's together. It is a happy life me da and mother have known together. So do not worry what folks may think if yar father decides to pay court to Janie. All that matters is what they think and feel."

"Yer right!" Adelaide agreed. She seemed thoughtful for a moment and then smiled at him, giggling, "And my daddy must be good at kissin'! For he sure turned Janie's head away from Harvey well enough!"

Chuckling, Chance agreed, "Aye! One kiss beneath the mistletoe the other night, and she has no more thoughts of Harvey."

Adelaide sighed, relieved that she was not the only one who had noticed the way Janie had dropped any thought of Harvey. And wouldn't it be wonderful if it truly would be Janie who healed Dean Plume's broken heart?

In fact, Adelaide felt so thoroughly giddy over the notion, she wanted to share more with Chance.

Therefore, she reined Georgie to a halt and asked Chance, "Would ya like to see Georgie's best trick?"

Chance's smile broadened as he reined in Paddy as well, answering, "Aye! What sort of trick have ye taught him?"

Adelaide proudly arched one eyebrow. "A very, very impressive one," she answered.

Dismounting, Adelaide proceeded to take the rope from her saddle and fashion it into a lasso. As Chance watched, she began to twirl the lasso, until it had enough momentum that she could leap in and out of its circle.

As Chance laughed with being entertained, even applauded as she hopped in and out of the lasso's spinning ring, Adelaide giggled and said, "Now…watch this."

Carefully she walked to stand in front of Georgie, all the while swirling the lasso. "Georgie Porgie? Do you want a turn?" Adelaide asked the horse. Immediately, the horse began to nod over and over and over in time with the rhythm with which the lasso's ring spun. "Then…here you go!" Adelaide giggled, as she transferred the top of the rope to be gripped between Georgie's teeth.

As Georgie's head bobbed to and fro in keeping the lasso spinning, Adelaide's heart swelled with delight as Chance exclaimed, "Whoa ho ho! He's doin' it! He's doin' a fine job at it too. I've not seen the like—not in all me livin' days, I haven't!"

Knowing Georgie would tire quickly, Adelaide said, "Good job, Georgie Porgie! Good job!" indicating the horse should stop the lasso. As he did, Adelaide gathered up the rope, returning it to its place.

Still laughing with astonished amusement, Chance offered, "A trick indeed, lassy! The best I've seen."

Adelaide giggled. "Well, my Georgie Porgie has worked very hard on learnin' it." She mounted, winked at Chance, and said, "That's why I always, always give him his favorite reward once he's finished performin' his trick."

"And what be his favorite reward?" Chance asked.

"A gallop, with a destination of his choosin'…" Adelaide began. "Or a race! On yer mark, get set, go!"

Chance smiled as Adelaide pressed Georgie's ribs with her stirrups, launching him into an immediate gallop. "Get on, Paddy!" Chance ordered, impressed by the lead Adelaide had before him.

Her horse was much faster at the get-go than he looked like he would be, and Adelaide's leaning low and forward gave the horse the necessary freedom it needed to race onward.

"Aye, Paddy!" Chance laughed, leaning low and forward in his own saddle. "She's a fine harsewoman; indeed, she is."

The pounding of hooves, the strains of leather, and the cool crisp air invigorated Chance as he and Paddy began to close the distance, however slowly, between themselves and Adelaide.

Yet an instant later, Chance's joy and excitement vanished as he remembered there were thieves operating nearby, most likely outlaws who would as soon shoot a man who happened upon them as to look at him—do worse to a woman.

"Get on, Paddy!" Chance growled, spurring the horse to increase its speed. He had no idea where or how far Adelaide would ride before stopping—though he suspected the grove of ancient-looking cottonwood trees up ahead was her destination. After all, she was riding straight for it.

"Hup! Hup! Hup!" Chance shouted, and Paddy responded. As Chance advanced on Adelaide, he hollered, "Lass! Rein in! Rein in, lass!"

Chance exhaled a sigh of relief as Adelaide did indeed gradually slow her horse to a canter and then a trot.

Reining Paddy into a trot beside Georgie, Chance said, "Methinks 'twould be wise for us to remain closer to the ranch house and outbuildin's than further from it today." Chance didn't want to plant fear in Adelaide's mind, thereby tainting their ride together, but neither could he ignore the unseen threat that might be lurking in the pastures. Although it would take heartless outlaws indeed to rustle cattle on Christmas Day, he knew just *how* heartless bad men could be.

Adelaide smiled, reining Georgie to a walk. "Why?" she inquired. However, her smile disappeared as understanding was hers then. "Oh, I see," she sighed. "But, Chance, do ya really think whoever is takin' our cattle would steal more? I mean, it's Christmas Day! Surely even rustlers wouldn't..."

Chance shrugged.

Adelaide admitted, "Of course they would. In fact, what better day would there be to rustle cattle? After all, good folks are happy, enjoyin' the mornin' with their families." Adelaide exhaled a heavy sigh of discouragement and frowned for a moment. Still, even Chance's heart felt light, as she looked to him, smiled, and said, "Well, rustlers or not, we're out for a ride, and I'm determined to show ya my favorite hideaway."

Chance smiled, feeling somewhat relieved. At least she wasn't planning on riding straight out into the open beyond the grove. No one was certain exactly where the rustlers were snatching the cattle; the rustlers were better than he'd ever heard of at covering their tracks. But Chance figured the protection of the cottonwood grove would give him and Adelaide good protection even with being winter-barren of leaves. After all, the cottonwood trees' trunks were enormous and their limbs prolific. Even so, he was glad he'd brought extra ammunition for his rifle and pistols. Adelaide Plume was a brave little lass and would probably consider fearlessly riding out into the open in defiance of rustlers as a daring challenge. Thus, Chance was relieved that the cover of the cottonwoods was her intended destination.

"This is my favorite hideaway," Adelaide explained as she dismounted Georgie, plopping his reins haphazardly over a low tree limb. "Especially in summer and fall, of course."

"I've rested here many times meself, I have," Chance offered, dismounting and smoothing Paddy's nose. "'Tis a place of solitude and serenity, indeed."

"Oh, it is so dear to me," Adelaide sighed, smiling.

Chance's heart swelled inside his chest as he studied her—as he watched her hurry to a fallen tree trunk and sit down on it. Adelaide Plume was the most beautiful young woman Chance had ever set his eyes upon, and he determined then and there she would be his—much sooner than later. No matter what he needed to do to convince her father that Chance Flannery was worthy of Adelaide's hand, he would find a way to do it.

Striding to where Adelaide sat so properly on the fallen trunk, Chance smiled as he took his seat beside her—for the roses in her cheeks and the flash of favor in her eyes caused his knees to feel weak.

"It's beautiful, isn't it?" Adelaide asked Chance. "So quiet and solitary. Why, Roger and I have read and enjoyed many books in this quiet place. Although it does take us so long to arrive and then to return home." She giggled, adding, "Daddy and Pop have scolded me more than once for disappearin' for the whole day long. But this is where I go…mostly by myself. As I said, it takes Roger far too long to get here with his slow pace."

"So ye led me here to tell me the tales of ye and Roger and yar readin' of scandalous books, is it?" Chance inquired flirtatiously. "And I was thinkin' that it might be the broad bush of mistletoe hangin' high overhead of this spot that instigated our destination."

"What?" Adelaide gasped. She looked up, blushing when she saw that Chance was right. Nestled in the strong branches of another cottonwood whose limbs stretched well over the fallen trunk was an enormous growth of mistletoe, its greenery heaping with white berries.

"Oh…I didn't realize. I…I…" Adelaide stammered, looking back to see Chance staring at her—the enticing blue smolder in his eyes, a grin of pure seduction curving his tempting lips.

"Aye, ye did not," Chance said. His voice was low and alluring, like maple syrup poured over buttery flapjacks on a cold winter's morning. "And I tell ye this, Adelaide Plume," he continued, removing his gloves before reaching out and taking her face in his warm, strong hands. "I mean to pick that bush bare of berries on this Christmas Day, I do. I mean to have me fill of kissin' ya here and now. Far if Roger can have yar whole day long, I mean to have mine…but there'll be no readin'. That I promise ye."

As Chance leaned forward, kissing her tenderly, Adelaide's arms and legs went to jelly—poorly congealed jelly at that! As he deepened their kiss, coaxing her mouth to meet his in a mingling of such a rapturous exchange of affection, Adelaide exhaled the breath she'd been holding and wrapped her arms around his neck. Pulling herself against him, she sighed again, happy in being the one place she would rather be more than anywhere in all the world—bound in the arms of Chance Flannery!

After several long, very long moments of blended mouths and exchanged passion, Chance broke the seal of their kiss and leaned back just a little, grinning at Adelaide and saying, "That'd be worth the pluckin' of one berry." He reached out, caressing her cheek with the back of his hand as he gazed at her. "But as I said before…I mean to pick that bush bare today, lass."

Melting into his arms, Adelaide pulled his head to hers, capturing his lips with her own, in silent begging for more of the warm, exquisite nectar of his profoundly proficient kiss. And Chance did not hesitate in granting her what she wanted. Instead, the passion that ignited between them, there in the cottonwood grove on Christmas morning, was so intoxicating, a brief thought flitted through Adelaide's mind concerning her knowledge of a deeper intimacy that was shared between a man and a woman—a husband and a wife.

In all her life she'd imagined the intimacy required in marriage, and as a necessity for having children, not only frightening but also repugnant to even think upon. Until those moments there, under the mistletoe, kissing Chance. Then and only then could she understand why God had created such an attraction between a woman and a man. The overpowering love in her heart for Chance, and the desire in her body for an even more intimate closeness with him, caused her fear and detestation of what little she did understand about the physical intimacy of marriage to vanish.

Suddenly, and very unexpectedly, Chance pulled back slightly. "Did ye hear that?" he asked in a whisper.

Adelaide had heard nothing, for the ringing in her ears caused by the bliss of Chance's kiss was nearly deafening.

"No. What do ya think ya heard?"

"Shh," Chance whispered, scowling as he released Adelaide, quietly leapt up, and crept back to his horse. Mouthing, *Shh*, to her again, he gestured to her that she should get down off the tree trunk they had been sitting on and lower herself in front of it.

As Chance carefully made his way back to her, his rifle and two boxes of cartridges in hand—as he knelt down in front of the large old trunk, propping his elbow on it as he peered through the foliage to the pasture beyond, Adelaide did hear something. Voices!

Turning on her knees to follow Chance's gaze, Adelaide covered her mouth to silence her gasp of astonishment as she saw the men—four men stealthily herding six head of cattle.

Leaning close to Chance, Adelaide whispered, "Two of them were at the Christmas bazaar and dance, remember? The brothers scoutin' out land for their pa…or so they claimed."

"Aye," Chance agreed in a whisper. "Looks more like they be scoutin' out yar da's cattle, as well as Mr. Worden's, it does."

Adelaide nodded, noting that three of the head were branded with the Plume mark and three with Mr. Worden's. She frowned, angry that Bill Burlinson and his brother had been so brazen as to attend the Christmas festivities held in Oak Creek.

"And to think I accepted a dance with that man," she breathed. "A waltz, in fact. Why, I could just—"

But her words were silenced as Chance placed an index finger to his lips, indicating she should be quiet.

And he was right! Bill Burlinson himself had turned his horse in the direction of the cottonwood grove. He sat still in his saddle, frowning, and raised an arm to his fellow outlaws to hush them.

Chance leaned over, placing his lips to Adelaide's ear. "Ya must get on Georgie and ride, Adelaide. Ride like the wind to the ranch house and tell Ike and the others what's happenin'. There's to be shootin' far sure and far certain here, and I want ye as far away from it and as fast as ye are able. Now go!"

As tears began to brim in her eyes, Adelaide opened her mouth to argue. She couldn't leave Chance to face four rustlers! It would take her far too long to ride back to the ranch—no matter how fast Georgie carried her!

She heard an all-too-familiar click and looked back to the place where Bill Burlinson sat astride his horse. Sure enough, Bill had drawn his pistol and was aiming it toward the grove of trees!

"Get down!" Chance said a moment before a shot rang out.

Bill's first shot hit the old tree stump—Adelaide felt it hit.

"Go! But stay low!" Chance growled as he took aim and fired.

As Adelaide began crawling back toward Georgie, thankful that her daddy had taught her to train every horse she had ever owned to stay put at the sound of gunfire, she heard Bill cuss and begin hollering to the other men that he'd been hit. Georgie had startled at the shots, of course, but he stood his ground.

More shots rang out, and Adelaide knew Chance was outnumbered. Still, she heard his rifle repeat—heard the rustlers begin hollering—and she hoped the gunfire would be heard by the Plume men who were out riding the fence lines and draw them to the cottonwood grove to help Chance.

Yet as she reached Georgie—as she began to mount—her attention fell to her own rifle: the 1873 lever-action repeating rifle that had belonged to her mother, its leather scabbard attached to her saddle. Adelaide never rode out without it; her daddy had taught her that too.

In that instant she realized that no matter how good a shot Chance was, he was outnumbered. Even if her daddy, pop, and brothers heard the shots, she had no idea how far away they were. It would take her too long to fetch help.

And so drawing her rifle from its scabbard and grabbing a box of cartridges from her saddlebag, Adelaide dropped back to the ground instead of mounting Georgie. As she quickly returned to Chance, he frowned when she sat down next to him in the protection of the tree trunk.

"Lass! I told ye to—" he began.

A bullet whizzed overhead, and Adelaide turned, taking aim over the top of the stump.

"It'll take far too long to bring help from the ranch," she noted. "Of course, I'm sure ya know that. But I'm not gonna leave you here alone with four men shootin' to yer one!"

Pulling the Winchester's trigger, Adelaide triumphantly arched an eyebrow at Chance when she saw one of the men grab his left arm and swear. "I'm a good shot too, ya know," she pointed out.

Chance's frown slowly faded as he grinned with approval and admiration. "Aye, I did not doubt it for a moment," he said as another shot hissed overhead. "Stay low," Chance instructed. "Try to count their shots, and rise when ye think they are in need of reloadin'."

"Aye, me laddie," Adelaide said, sinking down below the top of the old tree trunk as a bevy of bullets were fired.

The sound of an approaching rider from the direction from whence she and Chance had come startled them both, and they turned, ready to fire.

"Whoa! Hold up!" Harvey shouted as he reined to a stop.

It was the first time in years that Adelaide was actually glad to see her older skunk of a brother.

"The rustlers it be," Chance hollered. "And ya'll never believe who two of them—"

Just as Harvey had dismounted and was drawing his own rifle from his scabbard, more shots rang out. Adelaide gasped as Harvey clutched his chest and collapsed to his knees.

"Harvey!" Adelaide cried out.

But Harvey shook his head, removing his hand from his fresh wound to inspect it. "I'm hit…but not bad," he assured her. Crawling to join Chance and Adelaide behind the fallen tree, Harvey took aim and fired, dropping down behind the trunk, the bleeding at his shoulder increasing.

Furious that rustlers were shooting at the man she loved, as well as having shot her brother, Adelaide waited for the pause in gunfire as Chance had instructed before peeking over the tree trunk and firing. One of the men she had never seen before that day swore and leveled his pistol in her direction.

"Pop and Fordy ain't far behind me," Harvey breathed. "We had just split up when I heard the gunfire."

Hope welled in Adelaide's bosom, knowing that between Chance, Pop, and Fordy, the rustlers didn't have a prayer of outgunning anyone.

Chance took aim, firing several shots in rapid succession. More shouting and cussing emanated from the direction of the rustlers as Chance ducked behind the tree trunk to reload.

"Rapid fire, lass," he instructed as he loaded his Winchester with fresh ammunition. "'Twill unnerve them. Don't take too much time in aimin' just now. Just fire off while I'm reloadin'."

Adelaide did as Chance instructed, and as Harvey pulled himself to his knees, joining Adelaide in rapidly firing at the rustlers, the outlaws' horses did indeed spook, sending three of the men tumbling from their saddles and their horses galloping off in every direction. Bill Burlinson was the only man left mounted, and Adelaide knew he had already been hit once in the arm.

However, just as Chance finished reloading his Winchester 1892, a bullet hummed past Adelaide's head. The bullet barely missed her; she knew it by the heated ringing in her right ear.

"What the hell?" Chance shouted, rising to his full height. "Stop shootin' at me woman, ye cowardly bastards!"

Adelaide watched in astonished horror as Chance leapt over the fallen cottonwood trunk, braced the butt of his rifle below his waist, and began firing like nothing Adelaide had ever seen. Somehow

Chance's rifle had been modified so that he only had to pump the lever by hand as he fired more rapidly than Adelaide thought possible.

Inconceivably, the three men who had been thrown from their horses all fell to the ground. Chance's speed with the weapon combined with the height at which he fired had peppered their legs, incapacitating them.

Although there was no way to count the bullets Chance had fired in such quick succession, Adelaide knew the rifle did not hold an infinite amount of ammunition. Quickly, she took aim at the one man who remained a threat: Bill Burlinson. Knowing her own weapon was low or nearly empty of ammunition because of rapid fire, she inhaled a deep breath and held it. Squeezing the trigger, she remained still until she saw Bill flinch—saw blood begin to ooze through his trousers at his knee.

"And to think I waltzed with you, you dirty, yellow…" Adelaide mumbled as she squeezed off what proved to be the last round in her rifle. The bullet hit him in the arm, but Bill Burlinson still managed to somehow reload one of his pistols.

Adelaide screamed, "No!" as she watched Bill level the pistol in Chance's direction. But Chance tossed his empty rifle aside, drawing his own pistol with such lightning speed, Bill Burlinson was dead before he'd had the chance to trigger.

Adelaide watched in stunned silence as Chance walked over to Bill Burlinson, kicking his lifeless leg twice.

"Them rustlers riled up the wrong Irishman, I'd say," Harvey puffed.

"Don't a one of ye bastards move," Chance growled as one of the men lying on the ground raised his pistol. "Or I'll spill yar brains here and now, I will."

Chance cocked his pistol as he aimed it at the man's head, just as the drumming of hooves sounded from the west.

Tears spilled over Adelaide's cheeks as she saw Pop, her daddy, Fordy, and Mr. Worden rein in near the half-dead men, rifles drawn.

"Where's Adelaide?" Dean asked at once.

"Behind the old tree trunk there, she is," Chance answered. "Harvey too. He's been shot, but not fatally." Looking up to Mr. Worden, Chance added, "The cattle scattered when the shots were flyin' by, they did, Mr. Worden. I counted three of them as yars."

"Thank ya, son," Mr. Worden said with a nod.

"Ya know yer bleedin' there, Chance...don't ya?" Fordy inquired, pointing to Chance's leg.

"I did not know it," Chance admitted as he looked down to see blood soaking his trousers at his left thigh.

"And...uh...there too," Fordy added, indicating Chance's left arm.

"Hmm," Chance hummed as if it were no more than a mosquito bite.

"Hmm?" Adelaide growled, leaping to her feet and crawling over the tree trunk. "You've been shot, and all you can say is *hmm*?"

She marched toward him intently, furious that he should act so nonchalant at having been shot—twice!

"Addy, darlin'!" Dean Plume called, dismounting and striding toward Adelaide.

"I'm fine, Daddy," Adelaide assured her father as he stopped her advance on Chance to embrace her. "I really am." She returned her father's hug, joyous in the strong, loving protection of it. "But Harvey's been shot...and apparently worse than Mr. Flannery here."

"Let's round 'em up, Fordy," Pop laughed as the three still-living men writhing on the ground moaned in pain. "I'm just glad yer all right," Dean sighed, holding Adelaide away from him as he studied her from head to toe.

"I'm right as rain, Daddy," Adelaide reassured him with a smile. She held up her mother's Winchester 1873. "Thank you for teachin' me how to shoot…and to never ride out without this."

Dean exhaled a deep sigh of relief, embracing Adelaide once more before chuckling, "Now you go tan Chance Flannery's hide for walkin' out to confront four men on his own, all right?"

"Oh, believe me, I mean to," Adelaide stated as a frown puckered her brow. "Chance Flannery!" she hollered. "Don't you ever, ever, *ever* do somethin' like that again!"

Chance turned to her, scowling. "I told ya to ride free of it all, lass," he growled.

Moments later, Chance and Adelaide stood face to face, scolding one another for what the other did or did not do to remain as safe as possible.

When Chance stopped reprimanding her long enough to take new breath, Adelaide plowed forward, "And I know yer mad at me for not ridin' off…but how could I? Don't ya know me at all? After everything and all yer reassurances that I should be myself…be true to who I am? Don't you know—"

She stopped speaking when Chance reached out, placing a hand over her mouth. "Don't I know by now that me own beautiful Adelaide is no shrinkin' violet?"

"Exactly," Adelaide affirmed as Chance's hand left her mouth— as he reached out, taking her rifle from her hand and tossing it to the ground next to his own—as he gathered her in his arms, gazing down into her eyes with the smoldering blue of his.

"Aye, I do know it," Chance admitted. "It scares the livin' life out of me, indeed it does. But I *do* know it. And I love ye for it all the more, lassy."

Adelaide's breath caught in her throat. Her eyes filled with hot tears.

"Wh-what did you say?" she whispered.

"I said I love ye, lass," Chance repeated. "I love *you*, Adelaide Plume. And I mean to have ye…to wed ye…to make ye my own."

He pulled her against his powerful, capable, muscular body then—kissing her with such a ravenous depth, she thought she might swoon.

Adelaide was lost in the waves of bliss crashing over her in those moments—bliss spurred by loving Chance and knowing for certain that he loved her in return—bliss in the feel of his arms around her and the promises he'd spoken.

"You do know the man is bleedin' dry standin' there sparkin' with ya, don't you, sweet pea?"

It was Pop's voice reminding her that Chance was indeed wounded that pulled Adelaide from her blissful euphoria.

"Yer wounds need to be tended, me laddie," Adelaide whispered against his lips.

"Perhaps," Chance mumbled against hers. "But I'd rather finish picking bare that mistletoe back there instead."

"Come along, you two smoochin' lovebirds," Dean laughed as he emerged from the cottonwood grove, leading Georgie, Paddy, and Harvey's horse with Harvey mounted on it. "Everybody's bleedin' all over everything. And someone needs to fetch a wagon and the sheriff."

Adelaide smiled at Chance as he smiled at her. "I love you, Chance. So much more than you can ever imagine."

"Oh, lassy," Chance said, his voice low and alluring the way Adelaide most preferred. He caressed her cheek with the back of his hand. "If only ye knew how completely me heart is yars, love."

"Blood…everywhere. Filthy, thievin' bastards lyin' out all over the ground here…" Dean reminded.

"Seems that big bunch of mistletoe and berries will have to wait," Chance said, winking at her. "For now."

♥

Adelaide sighed as she closed the book and set it down in the straw next to her.

"I've heard it was an adventurous readin' indeed…*The Swiss Family Robinson*," Chance commented. "But it seems to me that Roger was somewhat disinterested in that last chapter, he was."

Adelaide giggled as she lay against Roger's back, Chance next to her. "Well, I have read it to him before. That's probably why he slept through most of it. That and the fact that I saved the last of the Christmas cookies for you."

"Aye, but *I'm* interested, and I'm more shot up than Roger be— so maybe just a bit more deservin' of the last of yar delicious cookies, hmm?" Chance teased, leaning over to kiss Adelaide's cheek. "And the lad will have to learn to share yar attention, he will. Although I can well imagine how hard 'twill be for him."

Adelaide giggled, nestling against Chance's warm body.

"What a Christmas it has been," she sighed. "A beautiful day…yet fraught with danger and harm." Her eyes filled with tears as she thought of the wounds Chance was nursing—of how miserable Harvey's wound was, being even worse than Chance's. Even a skunk like Harvey didn't deserve to be shot.

"I still cannot believe I waltzed with that rustlin' outlaw," Adelaide groaned.

" 'Twas brazen of them Burlinson brothers to attend the Christmas festivities in town, it was," Chance grumbled, "all the while stealing cattle from yar family and Mr. Worden so that their da could come and bully, in hopes they would sell to him and his odious big ranchin' ways. The sheriff says that their da will be punished as well for his part in it...his contrivin' of it."

Adelaide exhaled a heavy sigh, trying to fight off the discouragement that was endeavoring to impede her happiness.

"Pop says that someday it'll only be big ranches like the ones Mr. Burlinson owns. That the big dogs will push and terrorize other ranchers until they have no choice but to fold," she mumbled.

"Aye. And it may well be yar pop is right, lassy," Chance sighed. "'Tis unfortunate that change comes...that it always will." He rolled to his side, hovering over her then, gazing down into her eyes with such intense and obvious love in his own that tears again threatened to spill over onto her cheeks. "Yet I can promise ye that there is one thing so constant and true, so unwaverin', permanent, and everlastin' that it will never change...not now, not forever," Chance offered, brushing a stray strand of hair from her forehead.

"And what might that be, Mr. Chance Flannery?" Adelaide prodded.

"That I love ye, Adelaide lass," he whispered. "That ye are dearer to me than me own life, ye are. And that when we are wed— and we will be wed soon—I will love ye beyond anything any woman on earth has ever known."

Adelaide reached up, tenderly caressing the back of his neck with her fingers before letting them weave through the softness of his hair.

"Even though I'm not a shrinkin' violet...all prim and proper and—"

Chance covered her mouth with his hand. "Most especially because ye are not a shrinkin' violet."

He kissed her—his lips warm, his mouth hot and demanding.

"Although ye do smell of violets, me lass," he mumbled against her mouth. "Smell of violets, taste of nectar and Christmas cookies."

Adelaide giggled, delighted by his loving, flattering words.

"And now," Chance said in his low, provocative, maple-syrup-over-warm-buttered-flapjacks voice. "We shall pluck the bush bare of berries here and now…before Roger and the rest of the world."

"What berries?" Adelaide asked, smiling with delight.

"The berries on the sprig of mistletoe that Roger gathered far us earlier," Chance answered.

Adelaide's brow puckered with puzzlement. Nevertheless, as Chance pointed one index finger upward at the ceiling of the barn— as Adelaide glanced up to see a large bouquet of mistletoe hanging directly above their heads—she burst into giggles.

Wrapping her arms around Chance's neck and pulling him to her, Adelaide kissed him sweetly on the mouth before asking, "And aren't you glad that we have such a thoughtful and talented pet such as Roger, my love?"

"Aye, lass. Indeed I am," Chance breathed a moment before his mouth descended to hers.

And as their kisses blended with infinite love and impassioned desire, the moonlight cascading through the barn window bathed them in such luminous wonder and beauty that Roger himself glanced up to the moon, nodding—as if in response to angels who whispered through that window to heaven that all was just as it should be on that Christmas night of gossamer moonlight and berry-laden mistletoe.

EPILOGUE

The sun shone warm and bright, and not one cloud nested in the clear sky to impede its radiant promise of beautiful mid-June summer's day. The wildflowers bloomed in prolific yellows, lavenders, and pinks seamlessly in tandem with the rich, green pasture grass, and songbirds trilled from their perches in nearby trees and on the rooftop of the Plume ranch house, as if they themselves were honored guests that day as well. Even Roger was bedecked with lengthy garlands of fresh flowers and greenery festooning his long horns, so that everyone and everything stood in happiness and favor of the bride and groom.

"I now pronounce you man and wife," the thin, lanky preacher announced. "You may kiss the bride," he added to the groom with a cheerful wink.

As the groom was not at all shy, he gathered his lovely bride into his arms, capturing her mouth in a ravenous kiss seldom seen in public, sending the wedding attendees applauding and cheering with approval, as well as gladness for the couple.

"They say that June brides are brides forever," Adelaide said to Chance as she applauded her father's fearlessness in smothering his new wife with kisses in front of the whole of Oak Creek that had been invited to the ranch to celebrate the wedding.

Chance's dark brows puckered, and he asked, "And what be the meanin' of that? How be June brides any different from any other bride? Far instance, a February bride, hmm?" He winked at Adelaide, and her heart fluttered, just as it had every time he winked at her from the very moment he first had—especially since their wedding night in February, the very thought of which caused a blush to rise to her cheeks even in that moment.

Adelaide shrugged. "Oh, somethin' about the Roman goddess Juno, the goddess of marriage…and how women who marry in June are supposed to be blessed with more prosperity or some such nonsense," she explained.

"'Tis nonsense indeed, it is," Chance agreed. Taking hold of Adelaide's shoulders, he turned her to face him. "Methinks it is the February bride that will be the happiest farever, I do."

Adelaide smiled, her heart hammering in her bosom, for her love for her husband had only grown since she and Chance had wed—something she would've thought impossible! But it was true; with each passing day, no matter what life tossed at them, Adelaide loved Chance more.

"I agree," she said, rising on her toes and pressing a warm kiss to his lips.

As butterflies took to madly flapping in her stomach, she reached up, tousling Chance's dark hair.

"But I do know that my daddy will make Janie as happy as you've made me, darlin'," she told him, "if that's even possible. Still, if it is…Janie will be the second happiest woman on earth."

"Hmm. Is that so, lass?" Chance asked. His hands went to Adelaide's waist, his mouth seizing hers in a kiss that would've had the elderly ladies of Oak Creek gasping in horrified disapproval.

But being that everyone's attention was held by the newest bride and groom at the Plume Ranch, and that the groom was currently announcing that the dancing would begin shortly and that the foodstuffs were ready for enjoying, Chance and Adelaide continued their passionate exchange of loving affection.

"Thata boy, Chance," Fordy chuckled as he, Sylvia Anderson, and Harvey passed on their way to the food tables Mrs. Morgan had arranged.

"Gotta keep that fire lit, cowboy," Harvey added with a friendly smirk.

"Oh, I intend to," Chance chuckled.

Adelaide brushed a stray hair from her cheek, blushing as Chance winked at her.

"Ye know somethin', me lassy," Chance began as he strode to where Roger stood, flower-adorned and grazing.

"No. What?" Adelaide answered, smiling as she watched Chance tug at Roger's head so that he turned and began slowly ambling toward Adelaide.

"Methinks we've seen the weddin' of yar father and yar friend," Chance continued. Taking Adelaide's waist, he effortlessly lifted her to sitting on Roger's back. "And now it be time for a stroll. I was thinkin' to the willow tree just beyond the barn, I was. For the grass is cool and plush beneath its shade…a comfortable place for Roger to nap indeed."

"The willow, hmm? For Roger's sake, is it?" Adelaide giggled.

"Aye, for Roger's sake," Chance assured her, feigning concern for their pet steer. "After all, the beast has been quite nearly accosted today with so many people payin' him compliments, he has. A man can only endure so much attention of the sort."

Chance prodded Roger, "Move on, Roger. Move on," and the steer began moseying in the direction of the willow, his massive horns swaying back and forth, sending flower petals and leaves fluttering to the ground with each heavy step.

"And our destination of the willow has nothin' at all to do with the fact that Harvey mentioned he found mistletoe growin' in it last week, hmm?" Adelaide baited.

"Oh, not in the least, me dear, me darlin'," Chance answered, again feigning innocence. "It is only I miss the willow's long, slender branches that hang almost to the ground from its lowest limbs, I do. The privacy the willow offers is unmatched by any other tree I've known. And since yar pop and me purchased Worden's ranch—which I now point out to ye has no willow near the house—I thought ye and me might enjoy its refreshin' shade a bit now…whilst everyone else is occupied with yar father and Janie's nuptial celebration."

Adelaide's heart began to race, and her cheeks bloomed with a rosy blush. For she well knew what Chance's intention was. Before Pop and Chance had purchased the Worden ranch from Mr. Worden three months past—the rustling incident at Christmas causing Mr. Worden to tire quickly of cattle ranching—the enormous willow tree beyond the barn had been Chance and Adelaide's secret, secluded refuge from Adelaide's family. Indeed, the first month of their marriage, it had been the only place where they felt truly isolated in only each other's company.

Of course, now they owned and lived very comfortably in the Worden ranch house—Chance and his own crew of cowboys running the ranch and Pop enjoying his share of the spoils of the labor.

Still, the willow would forever hold a special place in Adelaide's heart. For she and Chance had shared a myriad of intimate moments while hidden away beneath the beautiful green canopy it afforded.

Indeed, it did not take long for Roger—even with his slow pace—to reach the old willow. And once Chance had lifted Adelaide down from Roger's back and seen the steer comfortably settled in the grass, he took Adelaide's hand, leading her to the other side of the tree trunk.

"Now, then, me beautiful lass," Chance began, taking Adelaide's face between his warm, strong hands and gazing down into her eyes. "'Tis time for the provin', it is."

He kissed her firmly, the moisture of his mouth promising hers that passion was to overtake her once more.

"The provin' of what?" she asked breathlessly between kisses.

"Why, the provin' to ye that the February bride is farever more the bride than the June one be," he mumbled against her lips. "Far me heart is constant full of me love far ye, Adelaide Flannery. And me body in endless want of yars."

Gasping in feigning the need for propriety in conversation, Adelaide covered Chance's lips with her fingertips, giggling when he began kissing them.

"So…am I to understand that you mean to pluck the mistletoe affixed overhead…you mean to pluck it bare of berries today? Hmm?" she flirted.

And as Chance pulled at his tie to loosen it—as the blue smolder of his eyes answered her already—he said, "There be no mistletoe in the willow, love. I only told ye there was to lure ye here so that I might have me way with ye."

"Then have yer way with me, my love," Adelaide whispered as Chance gathered her into his arms. "For I am and forever will be the most blessed and happiest bride the world has ever known."

As Chance's mouth descended, claiming hers with a demanding thirst that caused Adelaide's toes to curl, she thought for a moment she would tell him her secret then—before the intensity of their affection progressed. Nevertheless, she decided to wait—wait until their shared passion had been spent and Chance's mind was most blissful. Then she would tell him. When they were lying in the grass beneath the old willow together afterward, discussing lighthearted things and wishing all the best for her father and Janie—that was when she would tell him how truly thankful they would be at Thanksgiving dinner in November. For the doctor estimated their baby would arrive well before that special day of recognizing blessings with festive gratitude and feasting.

"Oh, how I love ye, lass," Chance mumbled a moment before he pulled them down into the cool grass beneath the willow tree. "How in love with ye I am."

Taking his handsome face between her small hands, Adelaide gazed into the smoldering blue of his eyes. "Oh, how I love *you*, impish lad that ye are," she giggled in a whisper, and imitating his brogue. "Lurin' me here beneath the willow…and when me own father has just been married," she teased.

"Aye, but believe me, darlin'," Chance chuckled. "Yar da has other things on his mind today, he does. And so have I."

Thus, as Chance continued to rain adoration, love, and pleasure over Adelaide's mind and body, she thought for a moment of the moon she so cherished. Vowing that that very night she would linger in the swing on the front porch in the blissful company of her handsome, beloved husband, gazing up into the perfect pearlized sphere of that window in the heavens, she would thank whoever was looking down on her. Whether it be her mother, her grandmother, or every angelic ancestor who knew her, Adelaide would tell them of her gratitude—for her birth—for who she was and being no shrinking violet. She would thank them for giving her the fortitude to chase happiness and win her true love's heart. As Chance kissed her there beneath he willow—caressed her cheeks, her arms, her shoulders—Adelaide surrendered to her endless love and desire for her bridegroom.

"Aye," she sighed, smiling with contentment. "And with not a sprig of mistletoe in sight."

AUTHOR'S NOTE

"Marley was dead, to begin with."

Ha ha! I sat down to begin my Author's Note for *Moonlight and Mistletoe*, and the first sentence of Charles Dickens's *A Christmas Carol* kept popping into my mind. This is related how? By the fact that I'm beginning my author's note with this:

To begin with, *Moonlight and Mistletoe* is a book wherein the title kept leaping around in my mind long before the characters or story plot ever did! This is *not* the first time I've written a book around a title I like—nor will it be the last! (See snippets for a list of my books that were titled long before I had any idea what the book would be about.) In truth, I prefer to think of a title first, because in years past, whenever I would begin a book and then try to come up with a title, I struggled.

For instance, when I was well into writing *The Rogue Knight*, I could not, for the life of me, think of a title. Seriously! Nothing would come to me. And so in desperation I called my friend and began to tell her about the story.

"It's about a girl who is living under her wicked aunt's thumb and longs for escape," I explained. "And then this vagabond guy shows up one night, and he becomes like a servant and then helps the girl escape. Oh, and his name is Knight, by the way. *Anyway,*

Knight is hiding out from the fact that he is a rich guy, and he's very flirtatious and stuff—you know, kind of a rogue and all. But I have no idea what to title the book."

After I'd elucidated more of the plot, my friend was quiet a moment and then said, "Well, why don't you just call it, *The Rogue Knight?*"

(P.S. I *love* the word *elucidate*! I picked it up as a kid from Disney's animated version of *The Legend of Sleepy Hollow*. Brom Bones uses it in the song he sings about the Headless Horseman.)

The Rogue Knight? Simply *The Rogue Knight?* Does the word "duh" mean anything to you? Seriously! I did a forehead slap on myself! Still, this is just one example of how hard it is for me to choose a title *after* I've begun writing a book.

From that moment on, I've always tried to entitle the book before I begin it, or at least while I'm in the process of writing the first few chapters. It's better for me that way, and I find my creativity is far more stimulated when the title is set firm.

But as I said, I do love it most when the title comes to me first. And so *Moonlight and Mistletoe* is in the "title first, story later" category. (Marley was dead, to begin with. See? It sticks in your mind! Kind of like the song, "How Do You Solve a Problem Like Maria?" from the *Sound of Music*! They're both so relentless in reminding you of themselves!)

Anyway, now that you've finished this book, you've realized that *Moonlight and Mistletoe* was about Adelaide's journey to learning that she is no shrinking violet and was never meant to be—about her realization that she didn't have to change who she was to get her man. Of course, she did begin to dress more appropriately for her age but because she wanted to.

Herein is where I plug my soapbox: that a woman can be empowered, strong, and still very, very feminine—glamorous, emotional, whimsical, or softly feminine (e.g., Adelaide's Christmas dress and hair style, her tenderness and nurturing with and of Roger, her embroidery and love of cooking for her family, and her deep care and love for her mother's doll). *Moonlight and Mistletoe* wasn't so much about bad guys and shootouts but about Adelaide's personal journey to confidence in herself—and of course great kissing under mistletoe and out in the barn.

In truth, it is akin to a journey I've been traveling for years now—a journey that began with my once-confident self—who knew that, although I wasn't a super model or anything, I am a good person who makes wise decisions confidently—but then spiraled down, down, and down until I was a shell of who I used to be. Those closest to me would be able to tell you how lost my confidence in every area of my life had become—and I'm still struggling to recover it. But fear not! I am no longer circling the drain with that issue in myself but beginning to rise instead! Those around me who I trust and who know me best have been invaluable in helping me remember that I am a good, kind person who can overcome these past eight years of downward spiraling to find my confidence once more. And writing *Moonlight and Mistletoe* has been very helpful as well.

My cheering section was ever and always behind me, reassuring, "You can do this! Write what you want, and quit worrying about what one cranky Amazon reviewer might think! Write for yourself and your core readers the way you used to do before life was so heartbreaking, stressful, and demanding! You can do it!"

It's like I have a small crew of Janie Higginson clones around me, to encourage me, help me, and support me when I feel I can't keep standing another moment. I'm sure you have people in your life like Janie—and I know you're as grateful to your Janies as I am to mine.

(Marley was dead, to begin with.)

As you know, I don't really feel comfortable sharing so much of my personal life with you like this, but I have had so many friends contact me and let me know that my sharing my struggles in my Author's Notes has helped them in managing their own, and I felt I wanted to let you know how much I have missed the me who would've owned a pet steer, who would've read to it on Christmas Eve and fed it Christmas cookies—the me that used to make doll mattresses, pillows, and quilts for dolly cradles, even if it was just for my own grandchildren to play with. (I did manage to make a set for my granddaughter a few years ago!)

I have a wise, very wise friend (you know her as Jean, my inspiration for the bats in the attic in *The Light of the Lovers' Moon*) who once told me, "You can never go back to who you were before. You learn to like who you have become." I agree with Jean—and still, I know that it doesn't mean our entire character changes. We will be beaten down by the quicksand that is life, but we're still who we are at our soul's core, in spite of the ups and downs. And as we learn to lean back and float in the quicksand, we will heal, and we can recover. (Did you know that's how to survive quicksand? You can float on it!) Wounded and scarred though we may be—and it may take years, decades even—but we can heal. I do feel the beginnings of a healing process where my confidence is concerned, and although I know there will be more quicksand ahead, I do feel more and more each day that I will able to float and survive instead of being sucked down to the depths.

And now, having once again shared another secret struggle with you, I will cease in endeavoring to uplift and move on to my snippets. Personally, I love the snippets! They are fun for me, because I like to reminisce on what, who, and where inspired me along the way in writing a book. I hope you enjoy them! And thank you for your friendship, encouragement, and patient loyalty! Remember: float—don't sink!

Love to You,
Marcia Lynn McClure
(P.S. Marley was dead, to begin with.)

Snippet #1—Jane "Janie" Higginson. Yes! For those of you who know my darling, sweet, gorgeous friend and Party Posse member June Higginson—you are right! Jane "Janie" Higginson is a tribute to Jun. I sooo love June and have for so long! Thank you for inspiring me, Junie Bee! I love you!

Also, I always wanted Janie to end up with Dean, but I doubted myself for quite some time, worrying that readers would not like Janie marrying a man so much older than herself. I toyed with having her end up with Fordy, but that was *not* being true to Janie's character or myself. Thus, the more I thought about it, and the further I got into writing the book, the more I was determined to do what Janie truly wanted to do: win the heart of a *real* man! Therefore, for anyone out there who might think it's shocking, gross, or inappropriate for Janie and Dean to marry, I'll skip over the details—of the fact that I had a great-grandmother who married my great-grandfather when he was a decade older than she was and a great-aunt who married a man thirty-two years older than herself and the same age as her father—and go straight to a list of guys you may know who are the same age, or nearly the same age, as Dean Plume. Numero Uno: Jensen Ackles! (And yes, Dean Plume is named after Dean Winchester in the TV series *Supernatural*.) Next, Ryan Reynolds, David Beckham, Jason Momoa, Orlando Bloom, Benedict Cumberbatch, Jason Aldean, Luke Bryan, Michael Buble, Enrique Iglesias, David Harbour (Hop on *Stranger Things*), and Bradley Cooper! See? Janie did well for herself!

Snippet #2—One tender, fond memory I have of being a child, and even a young *tweenager*, is of the church Christmas bazaars that were held each year. Long ago, everyone at church would work on making things—embellished linens (like embroidered pillowcases), woodcarvings, baked goods—to be sold at the Christmas bazaar to raise money for church activities planned for the upcoming year. Well, the Christmas bazaar that I remember most was the one where I acquired a true treasure. An elderly man in our ward had made two wooden doll cradles. They were very simple but absolutely adorable and perfect for what I had dreamt of having for years—a bed for my Baby Tender Love doll! I had had my Baby Tender Love Doll as a child and had always cherished her. (I still cherish her!) The little cradles were perfect and cost only five dollars each. My sister was a little girl and first on the cradles-for-sale scene, and so she chose first, and I was so afraid someone else would snatch up the other one before I could get to it. But heaven was smiling on me that day (I think I was maybe twelve or thirteen), and I managed to procure the second cradle. Oh, how well my Baby Tender Love doll slept then, warm and cozy in her little cradle, an old pillowcase for her blanket. I loved and still love that cradle! However, during one of our cross-country moves years ago, one of the rockers was broken, and I was heartbroken. How grateful I am to my friend Rhonda (you know her as the inspiration for Miss Raynetta in *Dusty Britches*) for gasping in horror when I suggested I would have to simply throw my treasured cradle away. She assured me she could fix it for me, and *eureka*! She did! Some wood glue and vise clamps was all it took (I'm obviously not a woodworker of any kind) to save the little cradle. And now that beloved little cradle resides happily in the little bedroom our grandbabies sleep in when they spend the night. It's beloved and always has a dolly nestled in it. For over forty years the little cradle has been a treasure to me, and now you know from whence my inspiration came for Chance's little cradle and Adelaide's purchase of it.

Here are a few photos for fun. The first is of my very own Baby Tender Love doll, nestled in the Christmas bazaar cradle. I keep my doll cached away with another doll I have (more on that later), but as you can see in the next photo, I am a staunch believer that little boys and little girls should have access to baby dolls! My mom bought a baby doll for each of my sons when they were toddlers—for she knew it would make their hearts more tender. I have one or two to play with, along with a few others. I love to watch my grandchildren changing the doll's diaper, dressing them, talking to them—it makes my heart happy.

As a side note, when I have time (once every few years, ha ha!), I like to restore Baby Tender Love dolls. I've given one to my oldest granddaughter, let my grandbabies play with two or three, and plan to fix up one for my youngest granddaughter soon. (Diane Holgate—let me know if you would like one to restore! I have a bunch!)

However, not everyone is as fond of opening the closet in one of our bedrooms to see the eight Baby Tender Love dolls I have waiting to be refreshed! A couple of guests we've had have opened the closet without previous warning and nearly passed out with the—to some—gruesome sight! Ha ha!

Snippet #3—One of my mom's little catch phrases that I always thought was very visually illustrating was, "Curl up and die." If someone was really embarrassed publicly or something, Mom would feel so bad for them and say something like, "Oh, poor thing! She just looks like she just wants to curl up and die." Now, *people* don't *usually* curl up and die—well, I'm sure they do; some mummies are proof of that. However, when I think of something curling up and dying, I imagine spiders! You know how if something besides your shoe, flip-flop, or broom kills them—like when they just die from bug spray and stuff—they literally curl up and die! Except for black widows. You and I have discussed at length—especially in the Author's Note of *Sudden Storms*—my mother's fascination with black widow spiders. And although black widows are hard to kill with anything other than your shoe, flip-flop, or broom (I personally don't get close enough to a black widow spider to use one of those implements), if you spray them with a good aerosol hairspray, they *will* curl up so they will be incapacitated just long enough for you to use your shoe to "die" them. I always loved that phrase of my mom's.

Snippet #4—Barnum and Bailey. If you remember, and you might not, at one point in *Moonlight and Mistletoe*, Adelaide states that the Morgan boys are "more entertainin' than anything P.T. Barnum ever cooked up." Well, it wasn't until I was writing this book that I discovered that the Barnum and Bailey Circus (purchased by the Ringling Brothers in 1906 and merged into the Ringling Brothers Barnum and Bailey Circus in 1919) closed after their final show on May 12, 2017. What P.T. Barnum began 148 years ago is gone forever. Just one sentence in this book mentions Barnum—the perpetuator of the FeeJee Mermaid hoax and promoter of his half fifth cousin, twice removed, Charles Sherwood Stratton's rise to fame as General Tom Thumb—right or wrong, the exploits (literally exploits, being that he did exploit many, many people) of P.T. Barnum have always intrigued me. But as sadly and inevitably happens, P.T. Barnum's adventures, misdeeds to those less fortunate, good deeds to those in need, legacy for making the odd or fascinating available to the public, and extraordinary showmanship will be forgotten entirely in time. Although the 2017 movie *The Greatest Showman* was inspired by P.T. Barnum's life and a great success, P.T. Barnum will pass into a forgotten history all too soon. And so I just had to mention P.T. in this book—so that at least someone knows *I* remember.

Snippet #5—Mistletoe. As you should well know by now, Washington Irving is far and away my favorite author, and I am often miffed by the fact that others are credited with things he first brought to light, so to speak. One of those things is the tradition of kissing beneath the mistletoe. Did you know that it was Irving who told Americans of the tradition through his book *The Sketchbook of Geoffrey Crayon*? Well, you do now, right? (And how can you not love a character with the last name Crayon? Another whimsical wonder of Irving's!)

Oh sure, mistletoe is found in Norse and Druidic mythology. But it was Irving's Christmas spent in England that gives us our tradition of kissing beneath the mistletoe. It's just a little something I wanted to share with you, because I love the tradition, and I love Washington Irving! Therefore, read on—an excerpt from Irving's "Christmas Eve," included in *The Sketchbook of Geoffrey Crayon*:

> As we approached the house we heard the sound of music, and now and then a burst of laughter from one end of the building. This, Bracebridge said, must proceed from the servants' hall, where a great deal of revelry was permitted, and even encouraged, by the squire throughout the twelve days of Christmas, provided everything was done conformably to ancient usage. Here were kept up the old games of hoodman blind, shoe the wild mare, hot cockles, steal the white loaf, bob apple, and snap dragon; the Yule-clog and Christmas candle were regularly burnt, and the mistletoe with its white berries hung up, to the imminent peril of all the pretty housemaids... The mistletoe is still hung up in farm-houses and kitchens at Christmas, and the young men have the privilege of kissing the girls under it,

plucking each time a berry from the bush. When the berries are all plucked the privilege ceases.

Snippet #6—Fanny. For many, many, many years—in truth, for all of my childhood at home—my mom kept her own beloved baby doll safely tucked away in a green antique trunk. Nestled among other keepsakes (mostly linens at the time), my mother's doll resided in that old trunk for decades upon decades—and it completely freaked me out! How on earth could that baby breathe? I don't care if she was a delicate, aged composition doll (composition being a material made from sawdust, glue, and other stuff like cornstarch and wood flour)—that doll could not breathe in that stuffy old trunk! My mom's doll being trapped in the trunk had always bothered me—made me feel sympathetically claustrophobic—but add to that the fact that one of my little sister's favorite books was entitled *The Muffletumps—The Story of Four Dolls*, by Jan Wahl, all about these dolls that were packed away in this old trunk in the attic. But when summer came along and the family that owned them headed out on vacation, the dolls would climb out of the trunk and have a great time! They'd eat muffins and eggs, play the piano, and have a wonderful vacation of their own. And then, when summer was almost over, they'd crawl back into the trunk, and their limbs would start to ache and go stiff, and they'd be in there for months until summer was back. Horrifying, seriously! It's the stuff of Wes Craven, of Stephen King! Even ol' Alfie Hitchcock probably never did a dolls-in-the-trunk-that-come-to-life story. My nightmares about that book were terrifying and often. And the fact that my mom's poor baby doll was trapped in a trunk only haunted me more. Naturally, Mom understood and would periodically give me permission to take her dolly out of the trunk and let her open her eyes and breathe some fresh air now and then. But it still haunted me.

There are many, many treasures my mom gifted to me throughout her life: her unconditional love, her sweet and tender affection, the sound of her voice, the smile in her eyes, her unfathomable wisdom. And although her baby doll was not the kind of gift we all most cherish, I remember the deep, heartfelt relief and profound appreciation that washed over me the day my mom couldn't stand the idea of her doll not being able to breathe in that old green trunk either—and gave her to me.

I recognized how hard it was for my mother to give up that doll—how much she loved me, and how well she knew me, by entrusting it into my care. Mom knew that I saw her baby doll as something that had its own heart—its own little imaginary spirit— and she knew I would take care of it always. And I have! For years I always displayed it in an old trunk that sat open, displaying the art on the inside of the trunk and the quilts tucked neatly in its belly. The doll would sit comfortably inside the lid, where she fit perfectly and watched the goings-on of the day. Every night on my way up the stairs to go to bed, I'd gently lay her down and cover her with something so that she could sleep well—lifting her back up into a sitting position the next day. But no matter how tenderly I took care of her, the old composition baby doll that was going on eighty years old began to wear more and more, until one day I knew she needed a better place to rest. And so I tucked her neatly inside a vintage baby sleigh I had used as a Christmas decoration for many years, covered her up with my husband's soft baby quilt, and tucked her away in my closet, where I knew she could rest and yet breathe comfortably. A year or so later, I gussied up my own Baby Tender Love baby doll and nestled her in the sleigh with my mom's doll.

There they both slumber undisturbed and breathe peacefully. I went into my closet and sat them up for a moment today, just so I could take this photo to share with you! But now they're all tucked in again—my mom's doll in her little white bonnet, red and green Christmas dress, and soft rabbit fur cape for added warmth—and my Baby Tender Love, in a new yellow crocheted dress and bloomers, with her nylon hair kept in place as well as it can be by a light hair net.

And so now you know why Adelaide was so resolved to make her mother's doll, Fanny, as comfortable as she could possibly be. Because Adelaide and I both know that baby dolls are more than just sawdust and glue or vinyl and plastic. They're real, and they can't breathe in a trunk!

Snippet #7—The fact of it is this: my mom made the most delicious sugar cookies on the face of the earth! I think I have mentioned this before, but I felt it needed reminding because Mom's sugar cookies (and her cookie icing) coupled with something I saw while watching *The Great British Baking Show* inspired the cookie chandelier displayed and happily consumed at Oak Creek's

Christmas festivities in the big barn. If you're a fan of *The Great British Baking Show*, you may remember the episode wherein the bakers were asked to create a cookie chandelier. I myself had never heard of such a thing, let alone seen one. But once I *had* seen one, I was thoroughly inspired! I would *love* to make my own cookie chandelier one day using my mom's sugar cookie recipe. But since I'm not sure I'm going to be able to pull that off any Christmastime soon, I decided I must incorporate one into *Moonlight and Mistletoe*. And of course Adelaide was one of the three persons honored to present such delicious and beautiful cookies tied with ribbons to the chandelier because she used my mom's recipe!

Now, I do know that everyone has their own favorite sugar cookie recipe and that everyone knows theirs is the very best recipe ever. Still, if you want to taste a truly wonderful sugar cookie—and I admit that the frosting recipe my mom handed down to me is a big part of what makes them so very delicious—I'm going to share my mom's original sugar cookie and icing recipes here. You know, just in case you ever want to enter a contest for best cookies and have your cookies displayed on a cookie chandelier!

P.S. Thank you so very much to my darling, autumn angel, super puzzling pal Gina for introducing me to *The Great British Baking Show* this past autumn (2018) during our annual autumn retreat together!

Patsy and Adelaide's Perfect Sugar Cookie Dough
(I usually double this recipe in the very least!)

Ingredients:
½ cup butter (room temperature)
¾ cup *plus* 2 tablespoons sugar

1 egg
1 ½ teaspoons pure vanilla extract
4 teaspoons milk
2 cups flour
1 ½ teaspoons baking powder
¼ teaspoon salt

Using an electric mixer, cream butter and sugar together. Add the egg and mix well, then the milk and vanilla extract. In a separate bowl, sift flour, baking powder, and salt together. Gradually mix sifted dry ingredients into moist mixture. Dough should be sticky.

Chill the cookie dough for at least one hour. Roll out dough to approximately ¼-inch thickness and cut into shapes using cookie cutters or other cutting implements.

Place on parchment-papered cookie sheet and bake at 350°F for 5 to 8 minutes, until just barely done. When I do it correctly, there's not even any hint of light brown or tan around the edges.

*If you're worried about them not being done, just set your cookie sheet on the stovetop over your oven for several minutes. The added warmth from the oven will finish cooking your cookies, without overdoing it.

Patsy and Adelaide's Incredible Icing/Frosting
(This is a "let me estimate it" recipe—so go with your gut!)

Ingredients:

½ cup butter (room temperature)

¼ teaspoon pure vanilla extract

⅓ cup evaporated milk (Methinks this is the kicker for making the icing so delicious!)

2 to 4 cups powdered sugar (confectioners' sugar)

Food coloring and other cookie decorating items

Using an electric mixer, cream the butter. Add the evaporated milk and vanilla extract, and mix well. Begin by adding 1 cup or so of the powdered sugar, mixing well. Gradually add in more powdered sugar, always mixing thoroughly, until your icing holds a peak when you peak it with a fork or knife. Separate icing into separate bowls, and then add color. Always make sure your cookies are cooled before you begin icing them. I also find that the icing needs a few hours to set—maybe even overnight. Enjoy!

Note: My mom used this recipe all the while we were growing up. Every Valentine's Day, she would painstakingly cut out heart-shaped cookies, ice them with delicious pink frosting, and carefully package them for us to take to school for our classmates. I swear that these are the best tasting sugar cookies I've ever had. So many I've tasted have no flavor whatsoever, but these are good even without frosting! Furthermore, they're not hard and crumbly like some others. Double delicious!

Snippet #8—As pleased as punch. The phrase has always puzzled me. I mean, I never understood why punch was pleased, being that I thought of punch as only a beverage made from fruit juices, water, sugar, and sometimes spices. So when I used the phrase in this book,

I decided it was time to do a little digging. What did I find? Well, let's just say, I didn't see that coming at all!

The phrase finds its origins in the age-old puppet character, Mr. Punch—as in Punch and Judy. (Who knew?) The Punch and Judy is rooted from sixteenth century Italian "comedy of the profession," with Punch himself debuting in England in 1662. Judy was originally named Joan, but puppeteers found "Judy" was easier to pronounce in Punch's signature "swizzle" voice. As you know, Punch and Judy shows were ever prevalent throughout England and the colonies in the eighteenth and nineteenth centuries, especially during summertime on British and American beaches. Of course, the popularity of Punch and Judy shows began to decline in toward the end of the twentieth century because of their perceived political incorrectness. After all, Punch is a chauvinistic jerk.

But back to the phrase. "As pleased as Punch" didn't appear until the late 1700s to early 1800s. And even though the phrase was coined to mean "as proud as Punch" (which I think makes more sense), Charles Dickens interchanged the phrase here and there throughout some of his novels.

I, for one, never liked Punch and Judy—especially Punch. He was ugly and mean. And being that punch the beverage is something far more pleasing the Punch the ugly, mean, three-hundred-year-old puppet, I'll just keep thinking of punch the beverage whenever I hear the phrase. Still, it's fun to know the history behind it, isn't it?

Snippet #9—Why yes, Sylvia! The Sylvia Anderson that so captures Fordy Plume's attention and heart is an ode to *you*, my darling friend, Sylvia Anderson! (Note to reader: For years I called Sylvia by my nickname for her, Sly—only to find out that she didn't like being called Sly—even though I meant it as the tenderest endearment. But fear not! I've adopted another nickname for her—that being Slyvia (pronounced Sli-vee-uh). I mostly call her Sylvia now—at least when she's sitting next to me! Right, Slyvia? Love you, Sylvia/Slyvia!

Snippet #10—Here's a shocking tidbit for you: The summer we were to turn thirteen (I was still twelve when the event occurred for me), my best friend I had our very first lickery Frenchy kisses! I know, twelve? Ick! Now, I can't speak for my friend, but as for me—N-A-S-T-Y! As romantically as it was meant to be for me by my kisser boy—well, let's just say that all my heroines with whom I use the analogy of being slobbered all over by a hound dog are inspired by that first lickery kiss I received at the tender age of twelve. But fear not! The kisser who kissed me the summer I was twelve-turning-thirteen got another chance to try it out on me a year later—and, I'm pleased to report, ended up being pretty good at it after all. Ha ha! The secrets I am revealing tonight are evidence that I'm tired and should've stopped writing hours ago!

Snippet #11—Enjoy this recipe for Adelaide's (and my) Christmas Eve Fried Potatoes, Apples, and Onions. Warm and cozy, delicious and buttery—divine!

Fried Potatoes, Apples, and Onions

Ingredients:
4 large potatoes (peeled and sliced about ¼-inch thickness)
2 large apples (peeled and sliced about ¼-inch thickness)
1 medium onion (finely chopped)

Butter
Salt and pepper to taste

Melt butter in electric skillet. Layer potato slices, salt and pepper, apple slices, and onion slices, and then repeat until all ingredients are in skillet. Fry potatoes, apples, and onions together in butter, salt, and pepper, covered (I use my electric skillet), occasionally and carefully turning with a pancake-turner until tender and potatoes are nicely browning. Mmmmmm!

Note: This recipe was my mom's (Patsy C. States Reed). It one of my family's favorites!

Snippet #12—Bravo, Washington Irving, AGAIN! You guessed it! Good ol' Washington Irving is also responsible for our vision (or at least our Victorian vision) of St. Nicholas! I will not bore you with more historic details but will simply leave you with his description of our jolly old elf, from his work *Knickerbocker's History of New York*.

And the sage Oloffe dreamed a dream,—and lo, the good St. Nicholas came riding over the tops of the trees, in that self-same wagon wherein he brings his yearly presents to children, and he descended hard by where the heroes of Communipaw had made their late repast. And he lit his pipe by the fire, and sat himself down and smoked; and as he smoked, the smoke from his pipe ascended into the air and spread like a cloud overhead. And Oloffe bethought him, and he hastened and climbed up to the top of one of the tallest trees, and saw that the smoke spread over a great extent of country; and as he considered it more attentively, he fancied that the great volume of smoke assumed a variety of marvelous forms, where in dim obscurity he saw shadowed out palaces and domes and lofty spires, all of which lasted but a moment, and then faded away, until the whole rolled off, and nothing but the green woods were left. And when St. Nicholas had smoked his pipe, he twisted it in his hatband, and laying his finger beside his nose, gave the astonished Van Kortlandt a very significant look; then, mounting his wagon, he returned over the tree-tops and disappeared.

Where, oh where, would we be without the writings of Washington Irving?

Snippet #13—Chance's Awesome Rifle Skills. Have you ever seen the opening credits to an old 1958–1963 TV series *The Rifleman*, starring Chuck Connors? Well, whether or not you have, run on over to YouTube.com and watch *The Rifleman* intro. And that, my darlings, is how Chance rapid-shot at the rustlers when he got fed up with them shooting at his woman! Sweet, right? I even changed the date the book begins (from 1890 to 1892) so that it was possible for Chance to own the same Winchester Model 1892 like Chuck's. Of course, Chance had modified his Winchester, in much the same way as Chuck's character, Lucas McCain, had. I have always, always, *always* loved that *Rifleman* intro, for literally as long as I can remember! So see? *The Rifleman*—a visual demonstration of how truly Bad-A Chance is!

Snippet #14—Which came first? The title or the book? And, voila! Here's a list of the books I have written wherein the title popped into my kookie brain very often long before I began writing the book!

A Bargained-For Bride
Beneath the Honeysuckle Vine
A Better Reason to Fall in Love
The Bewitching of Amoretta Ipswich
The Chimney Sweep Charm
A Cowboy for Christmas
A Crimson Frost
Dusty Britches
The Fragrance of her Name
A Good-Lookin' Man
The Haunting of Autumn Lake
The Highwayman of Tanglewood
Kiss in the Dark
Kissing Cousins
The Light of the Lovers' Moon
The Moon of Painted Leaves
Moonlight and Mistletoe
The Object of His Affection
An Old-Fashioned Romance
The Pirate Ruse
The Prairie Prince
Romance in a Winter Wonderland
Saphyre Snow
Shackles of Honor
The Stone-Cold Heart of Valentine Briscoe
Take a Walk with Me
The Tide of the Mermaid Tears

The Time of Aspen Falls
The Trove of the Passion Room
The Visions of Ransom Lake
Weathered Too Young
The Whispered Kiss
The Wolf King

Snippet #15—Just in case you've forgotten, remember—Marley is dead, to begin with. (Tee hee!)

To my hero and inspiration…
Kevin from Heaven!

ABOUT THE AUTHOR

Marcia Lynn McClure's intoxicating succession of novels, novellas, and e-books—including *Shackles of Honor*, *The Windswept Flame*, *A Crimson Frost*, and *The Bewitching of Amoretta Ipswich*—has established her as one of the most favored and engaging authors of true romance. Her unprecedented forte in weaving captivating stories of western, medieval, regency, and contemporary amour void of brusque intimacy has earned her the title "The Queen of Kissing."

Marcia, who was born in Albuquerque, New Mexico, has spent her life intrigued with people, history, love, and romance. A wife, mother, grandmother, family historian, poet, and author, Marcia Lynn McClure spins her tales of splendor for the sake of offering respite through the beauty, mirth, and delight of a worthwhile and wonderful story.

BIBLIOGRAPHY

A Bargained-For Bride

Beneath the Honeysuckle Vine

A Better Reason to Fall in Love

The Bewitching of Amoretta Ipswich

Born for Thorton's Sake

The Chimney Sweep Charm

A Cowboy for Christmas

A Crimson Frost

Daydreams

Desert Fire

Divine Deception

Dusty Britches

The Fragrance of Her Name

The General's Ambition

A Good-Lookin' Man

The Groomsman

The Haunting of Autumn Lake

The Heavenly Surrender

The Highwayman of Tanglewood

Indebted Deliverance

Kiss in the Dark

Kissing Cousins

The Light of the Lovers' Moon

Love Me

The Man of Her Dreams

Midnight Masquerade

Moonlight and Mistletoe

The Object of His Affection

An Old-Fashioned Romance

One Classic Latin Lover, Please
The Pirate Ruse
The Prairie Prince
The Rogue Knight
Romance at the Christmas Tree Lot
Romance in a Winter Wonderland
Romance in Sleepy Hollow
The Romancing of Evangeline Ipswich
Romance with a Side of Green Chile
Saphyre Snow
The Secret Bliss of Calliope Ipswich
Shackles of Honor
The Stone-Cold Heart of Valentine Briscoe
Sudden Storms
Sweet Cherry Ray
Take a Walk with Me
The Tide of the Mermaid Tears
The Time of Aspen Falls
To Echo the Past
The Touch of Sage
The Trove of the Passion Room
The Unobtainable One
Untethered
The Visions of Ransom Lake
Weathered Too Young
The Whispered Kiss
With a Dreamboat in a Hammock
The Windswept Flame
The Wolf King